THE PET FINDERS CLUB

Disappearing Desert Kittens

BEN M. BAGLIO

A division of Hachette Children's Books

Special thanks to Lucy Courtenay

To the real Jim and Jane Tatford, with love

First published in the USA in 2005 by Scholastic Inc

First published in Great Britain in 2008 by Hodder Children's Books

1

ISBN 978 0 340 93136 3

Typeset in Weiss by Avon DataSet Ltd,
Bidford on Avon, Warwickshire

Printed in the UK by CPI Bookmarque, Croydon, CR0 4TD

The paper and board used in this paperback by Hodder Children's Books are natural recyclable products made from wood grown in sustainable forests. The manufacturing processes conform to the environmental regulations of the country of origin.

Hodder Children's Books
a division of Hachette Children's Books
338 Euston Road, London NW1 3BH
An Hachette Livre UK company

Chapter One

Andi Talbot took the small, square present from under the twinkling Christmas tree and placed it in her mother's hands. "I was saving this until last, Mum," she said. "It's from me and Buddy. Merry Christmas!"

The little tan-and-white terrier sitting at Andi's feet barked when he heard his name. Judy Talbot carefully unwrapped the gift. "Oh, Andi!' she exclaimed, staring at the plum-coloured velvet notebook. "I need a new diary for next year, and this will be perfect. And it's my favourite colour!" She reached over and hugged Andi tightly. "I can't believe you're going away for a week tomorrow," she said. "I know you'll have a wonderful time with your dad, but Buddy and I are really going to miss you."

Andi swallowed a lump in her throat. "It's only a week, Mum," she said. "I'll be back before you know it."

She hadn't seen her dad since the autumn, and couldn't wait to spend some time with him, but it was so difficult to leave her mum and Buddy, and her friends Tristan and Natalie behind – especially at Christmas. Andi's dad lived in Arizona, America. Andi had lived in America too, in Texas, until just over a year ago, when her parents separated. Her mum had got a new job in England and she, Andi and Buddy had moved to Aldcliffe, a suburb of Lancaster.

"Don't worry about us," Mrs Talbot said, reading the expression on Andi's face. "You just enjoy every second with your dad. I can't wait to hear all about Arizona when you get back."

"I'll send emails," Andi promised. "And you can use your new diary to write down everything while I'm away. I want to know what Buddy gets up to, and whether you see Natalie and Tristan, and what the weather's like. So when I come home it'll feel like I haven't missed anything at all!"

The doorbell rang, making Buddy jump up and start barking. Andi shushed him and ran to open the door. Natalie Lewis was standing on the porch, wearing a stylish trilby hat in red leopard-print fur and a pink suede jacket.

"Happy Christmas!" she grinned, giving Andi and

her mum a twirl. "Great outfit, don't you think? I know the hat doesn't really match the jacket, but I couldn't decide which one I wanted to wear first. They'll both look brilliant with my chaps the next time we go riding!"

Andi's dad had recently given her some riding lessons at Riverside Stables, just outside Aldcliffe. Natalie had joined in after getting to know Neil O'Connor, whose mum ran the stables.

"You'll definitely be bright enough to spot in the woods," Andi teased. "Come in, Nat. I want to show you my new trainers and this fantastic new bag Mum bought me for my trip."

"Have you packed already?" Natalie asked, sinking on to the Talbots' sofa. "I'm so jealous. You'll get a great tan." She bent down and examined the pale skin on her legs. "I look as though I've been under a rock for months."

The doorbell shrilled again. "Tristan's here!" Andi's mum called.

Tristan Saunders pulled off his green striped beanie and ran a hand through his red hair as he came into the living room. "Merry Christmas. I would have got here earlier but it took us for ever to finish dinner. Dean's Christmas pudding needed so much chewing, my jaws are tired!" He slumped dramatically on to the sofa next to Natalie. "OK, I want to hear everything about this trip – especially the part about the snakes you're going to see."

"It's winter in Arizona too, you know," Andi pointed out. "The snakes will be asleep."

"Well, I hope you're going to wake a few up," Tristan said. "You can't go all the way to Arizona and not see a rattlesnake."

Natalie rolled her eyes at Andi. Tristan had developed a passion for reptiles since he'd been helping out at the Aldcliffe pet shop, Paws for Thought, and sometimes it felt as though he'd rather have scales than skin.

"Imagine," Tristan went on wistfully. "Real live rattlers all round you. You'll practically be able to pick them up, there'll be so many."

"Thanks for that information, Tris," Andi said dryly. "I'll send you one instead of a postcard. Or I could bring home a boxful for your New Year's Eve party?"

Natalie threw a rubber bone for Buddy, and he brought it straight back to Andi, as if he somehow knew he wouldn't be able to play with her for a while. She reached down and fondled his soft brown ears.

I'll miss Nat and Tristan, but I'll miss you most of all, Bud, she thought.

"You will walk Buddy every day, won't you?" she anxiously asked her mum. "He'll get fat with all the leftover turkey."

Judy Talbot smiled. "Of course I will."

Tristan picked up some photos that were lying on the coffee table. "Is this your dad's flat?" he asked, admiring the sunny, white-painted block. "It looks terrific. I can't believe he found a place so quickly."

"Dad can't believe it either," Andi admitted. "One minute he was on an oil rig in the South China Sea, and the next he was told he had to be in Tucson two weeks later. He said that without the Internet to keep him in touch with the estate agents there, he'd be living in a tent!"

"You could have ended up camping," her mum joked, scooping up the torn wrapping paper and heading for the kitchen. "People pay good money for holidays like that."

Andi's parents were divorced, and her dad spent most of his time travelling round the world for his job. He and Andi's mum were still good friends, and he sent them postcards of all the places he visited. He hadn't worked in America for ages, but now he'd be advising an Arizona-based firm on importing and storing fuel. Tucson was still a long way from Aldcliffe, but it was closer than the South China Sea!

Natalie and Tristan only went home after Andi had promised to email every day from Arizona. She went to help her mum unload the dishwasher and, as she stacked the dishes in the cupboard, she stared out of the window at the back garden. Everything here was so fresh and cold – the way storybooks always said Christmas should be. Andi had loved every minute of it: the snowy mountains, the carol-singing wrapped up in her mum's cosy red scarf, mulled apple juice warming her cold fingers, the smell of pine needles and crackling logs in the fireplace. Christmas here had been very different to Christmas in Texas, where they used to sit on the sun deck with cold turkey sandwiches and watch the sun set over the sea. She wondered what Arizona at Christmas would be like. Even hotter than Texas, probably. Suddenly she felt a rush of excitement and almost dropped the dish she was holding.

In less than twenty-four hours, she'd be on her way to Arizona to see her dad!

* * *

"Ladies and gentlemen, we will be landing in ten minutes." Andi pulled off her headphones and listened as the captain's voice crackled into the cabin. "Please fasten your seatbelts."

She peered out of the plane window as they started to descend. The landscape below them looked wild and dramatic. The strong desert colours beyond the city almost hurt Andi's eyes: reds and oranges and yellows set against a deep-blue sky. The plane landed with a tiny bump and taxied to a halt. Shouldering her bag, Andi followed Marie, the air stewardess who had been assigned to take care of her on the flight, out to the waiting bus and then across the warm tarmac to the terminal. After Andi had passed through Security and collected her luggage, Marie said goodbye with a smile. Andi checked her watch, then looked round for her dad.

"Chauffeur service for Andi Talbot," said a deep voice behind her.

"Dad!" Andi squealed.

"I can't believe you got so big!" her dad said, giving her a warm hug. "I swear you've grown since the fall. What's your mum feeding you?"

"Plant food," Andi joked. "It makes you grow several inches in a week."

"Let me take a good look at you." Her dad put his hands on her shoulders and stared at her. "You look pale," he said finally. "The Arizona sun will soon change that!"

Andi looked up at him. "And you're so tanned!" she said. "I thought your job kept you too busy for sunbathing?"

"Let's just say I make the most of my free time," her dad replied with a grin. He took Andi's hand and they headed out of the air-conditioned airport and into the late afternoon light. It was sunny and warm and not too hot – Andi's idea of a perfect day.

Her dad lived on the edge of town about forty minutes from the airport. Andi recognized the neat white block of flats straight away from the photos. Palm trees shaded the garden and there was an inviting blue plunge pool on the deck. Hibiscus flowers drooped round the doorway and filled the air with fragrance. The sky was huge and wide and blue, and dusty orange mountains stood far away in the distance, their shadows stretching across the desert as the sun sank lower in the sky. Andi breathed in the warm, scented air.

"Do you like it?" Her dad was watching her.

"I'll get used to it, I suppose," Andi sighed.

Laughing, Mr Talbot draped an arm round her shoulders and led her inside. The floor was covered with red terracotta tiles and brightly-patterned rugs, and landscape photographs hung on the white walls. The living area was open plan, with large glass doors opening on to the deck.

"What's my room like?" Andi asked.

"That's part of your Christmas present," said her dad. He opened a door at the end of the hallway to reveal a small white room with an arched window. Light from the setting sun streamed in and made patterns on the tiled floor. There was a bed and a chest of drawers, and a matching wooden desk in one corner with a computer sitting on it. The light was gorgeous but the furniture was pretty bare, and the room didn't look cosy and lived-in like Andi's bedroom back home, where you could barely see the paint on the walls because of all the animal posters.

"It's . . . er . . . great," Andi said.

"No, it's not," her dad countered with a grin. "It's a blank canvas. I wanted to wait until you got here and let *you* personalize it. I want you to feel like it's a real home away from home and you're welcome here any time."

Andi spun round and beamed up at him. "Really?

That's a *great* Christmas present! Thank you!"

"I'll take you shopping tomorrow. We can get rugs, pictures, lamps – anything you like."

"Wow!" Andi gasped. "Anything?"

"You bet," her dad said, dropping a kiss on her forehead. "We'll take a walk around town a little later, so you can get your bearings and maybe pick up a few ideas for your room."

Automatically, Andi looked round for Buddy. If they were going out, he'd love to come too. Then she remembered: he was back in Aldcliffe with her mum. Her excitement dimmed a little as she thought about Buddy and Tristan and Natalie back home. What if someone needed the Pet Finders Club when she was away? The club had been Andi's idea; she had started it with the others after Buddy went missing. Thinking of Natalie and Tristan looking for missing pets without her suddenly made her feel very strange.

"Are you OK?" asked her dad, looking concerned.

Andi forced herself to smile. "I'm fine. I was just thinking about the Pet Finders Club."

"I'm sure Aldcliffe's missing guinea pigs can spare you for a week," her dad joked.

Andi frowned. "It's more than just guinea pigs, Dad," she said. "We've found reptiles and dogs and a pedigree cat. We even found that pony that went missing from the stables, remember?"

"That's great, honey," Mr Talbot said absently, heading into the kitchen. "Can I fix you a snack before we go out? You must be starving."

Andi felt a bit disappointed that her dad wasn't taking the Pet Finders Club seriously. *He doesn't mean to upset you*, she told herself. *He just doesn't understand how important it is*.

"Oh!" she exclaimed, distracted by the brightly-decorated cactus standing in the corner of the room. She hadn't spotted it on the way in because it had been hidden behind the open door. "Is this your Christmas tree, Dad?"

Her dad passed her a sandwich across the breakfast bar. "It's an Arizona tradition," he said. "We don't get fir trees around here, so we use what we have."

"Careful, Dad, you're sounding like a local already."

"I feel like one," her dad smiled. "I took this job because of the great vacations I used to have in Arizona when I was a kid. It's always been a special place for me."

Munching her sandwich, Andi fingered the sparkling decorations hanging from the fat, prickly leaves of the cactus. There were stars, and little woven baskets, and a straw angel sitting on the top. It was cute and quirky, and Andi thought it was pretty cool.

Her dad jingled his car keys. "Ready? Let's go exploring!"

It was a short drive to the local shops. Andi's dad parked the car beneath a palm tree, and they walked down the street together. Andi peered into each of the brightly-coloured shops – some painted red, or deep blue, or pink – at the rugs, jewellery, paper lanterns and delicately-woven baskets displayed in the windows. They passed food shops hung with strings of blazing red peppers; clothes shops with rails full of rainbow knit clothes and soft scarves; furniture shops and astrology shops, book shops and art galleries. Bright-red buses rumbled past every few minutes, and the air was full of the smell of spices and dust and incense.

They passed a pet shop, and Andi dragged her dad to a stop so she could gaze through the window. It reminded her of Paws for Thought. She took a deep breath of the familiar smell of sawdust and animal feed. Perhaps she should go in tomorrow and introduce herself, in case her pet-finding skills were needed while she was here!

"I'm just going to get a newspaper," her dad told

her, pointing to a shop on the other side of the road. "I won't be long. Will you be OK waiting here?"

Andi nodded. "Of course."

Feeling as if one arm was missing because Buddy wasn't with her, she looked round for people walking their dogs. The only animals she saw were a skinny sand-coloured cat slinking down an alleyway and a grey-muzzled dog walking slowly towards her. She reached out her hand and patted the dog on the head as he limped arthritically past.

"Hello there, old boy," she said, stroking the dog's raggedy ears. "You've found a nice place to retire. Lots of sunshine and loads of people to talk to."

There was no sign of the dog's owner. Andi wondered if he was lost or a stray. But the dog seemed perfectly content, as if he knew exactly where he was going. He regarded Andi for a moment, then lowered his head and continued on his way. As Andi watched him go, she felt numb with longing for Buddy. It looked like the people of Tucson didn't go in for pets. Perhaps a place like this wouldn't need a Pet Finders Club at all!

Chapter Two

Dear Mum and Buddy,
I got here OK, the flight was cool. Dad's flat is great! He's put a computer in my room so I can send you lots of emails (and get emails back too, of course!). My room is plain white at the moment, but Dad has told me I can decorate it any way I like. We had a walk round town this evening, and you wouldn't believe how colourful everything is. I think I'm going to decorate my room in bright colours like green and blue and yellow, to contrast with the red floor tiles. Dad's taking me shopping tomorrow.

Andi paused. She wanted a cactus in a deep-blue pot so she could imagine being outside in the golden desert. She had seen some beautiful wall hangings and rugs in shades of reds and blues and yellows, and a stack of gorgeous green baskets that would look great on the shelves above the desk.

She turned back to the keyboard.

Does it feel strange at home without me? I hope Buddy's not missing me too much and is eating OK. Did you take him for a walk today? I only saw one dog in town tonight. I don't think people in Tucson keep pets. In fact, there don't seem to be many animals at all! I haven't even seen a rabbit here for Buddy to chase. There are a few geckos, but I think they'd move too quickly for Bud.

A wave of homesickness hit Andi, and the computer screen went blurry.

She wiped her eyes crossly. There was no way she wasn't having a great time. Her dad had taken her to a Mexican restaurant for supper. They'd listened to a mariachi band and browsed the little street stalls that had sprung up under the palm trees when the sun went down. There was so much to tell her mum, but all she could write was stuff about Buddy. What was wrong with her?

"You're just tired," she said out loud. It was true. She'd

had a long day, and she'd been yawning ever since they left the restaurant. She turned back to the screen.

> Time for bed. It's been a hectic day. Send me an email as soon as you read this so I can read it first thing in the morning! I miss you and Bud heaps.
> Lots of love
> Andi xx

With a sigh, Andi sent the email and logged off. Leaning on the windowsill, she stared out at the black desert. There was no moon tonight, and the air was sharp and cold. The lights of Tucson twinkled and glimmered, stretching away into the distance, and Andi was struck by how much bigger than Aldcliffe it was. It felt weird, being in a huge city out in the middle of nowhere! Yawning again, she got into her pyjamas and padded to the bathroom to clean her teeth. After saying goodnight to her dad, she climbed underneath her quilt and lay on her back, gazing up at the ceiling and watching distant headlights swoosh through the shadows until she fell asleep.

In the morning, it took Andi a few moments to work out where she was. Outside, the sky was blue and the air was already beginning to heat up, and there was an appetizing smell wafting down the corridor from the kitchen.

"Breakfast in ten minutes!" her dad called. "Are you up yet?"

Andi jumped out of bed. "Have I got time to check my emails?" she asked, putting her head round her bedroom door.

"Sure," said her dad, expertly flipping a pancake. "Just remember that I might start eating your share."

There were two emails – one from her mum and one from Natalie. Curling her legs underneath her, Andi read the email from her mum first.

> You'll get this first thing in the morning, Andi – as you asked! We're OK and Buddy's fine. He ate a pair of your training socks yesterday afternoon. I expect he missed the smell of your feet!!

The rest of her mum's email was full of stories about Buddy, and she'd signed off with five kisses at the bottom. Andi turned to the email from Natalie. It was long and full of exclamation marks and capital letters, and sounded exactly as if Nat was there in the room talking to her.

Hi, Andi!

Remember the set of Obedience classes Mum gave Jet for Christmas? We took Jet this afternoon. First he wouldn't even go in the door but just barked at all the other dogs trying to get to the class, as though he was guarding the place or something. When he finally decided to go inside, he went straight up to Fisher – how totally BRILLIANT is it that Fisher Pearce teaches Basic Obedience?!! – and sniffed him in this really embarrassing place. I nearly DIED! But then Jet got really into it, and even learnt to sit on command!! I only had to lean on him a bit to make him do it. He's so clever that he practised all the way home, sitting down on the pavement and in the middle of the road even when I didn't ask him to!!!

Andi grinned. Feeling much more cheerful than the previous night, she had a quick shower and pulled on a lightweight T-shirt and her favourite pair of combats. It seemed strange to put on summer clothes after all the winter layers she'd had to wear in Aldcliffe at this time of year.

"It sounds like this Fisher Pearce guy has his work cut out with Jet," Mr Talbot observed when Andi told him about her emails. He put several pancakes on Andi's plate and they sat together in a sunny spot on the deck.

"If anyone can teach Jet, Fisher can," Andi told him, pouring a generous puddle of maple syrup on her pancakes. "He's the local RSPCA vet. We've got to know him quite well through all our pet-finding."

"You've got to know a lot of people through this pet-finding stuff from the sound of it," her dad commented. "Didn't you meet Natalie that way?"

Andi nodded. "She's a really good friend. It's weird to think that I wouldn't have been friends with her if our dogs hadn't gone missing at the same time."

"Another missing-dog mystery, solved by Andi Talbot," her dad teased. "Aldcliffe sounds like a pretty dangerous place for pets."

"Ha ha," Andi said, pulling a face at him. She was determined not to get upset by anything her dad said about the Pet Finders Club today.

"So, are you ready for our shopping spree?" Mr Talbot asked her as they cleared the plates.

"Definitely," Andi said, rinsing the frying pan and setting it upside down on the draining board. She scooped up her jacket and followed her dad to the door. "I saw some gorgeous things yesterday that I'd like to have a closer look at. I saw these beanbags, and a horse poster, and a couple of rugs, and there was a fantastic lamp in the window of this shop—"

Mr Talbot put up his hands. "I get the message," he said. "We'd better get started straight away if we're going to pick up all that lot!"

The shops were quieter than they had been the night before, with only a handful of people browsing. There was no sign of the mariachi band and the restaurants had their shutters up, although Andi could still smell fajitas in the air. The shops had their doors wide open, with baskets and clothes displayed enticingly on the pavement. Andi ran her hand across a pile of rugs covered with intricate designs and admired a Navajo woman dressed traditionally in a velvet shirt, long skirt and petticoats, with a colourful blanket round her shoulders like a poncho.

"Do you mind if we go in here?" Mr Talbot indicated a small art gallery hung with bright oil paintings.

Andi glanced in the window and suppressed a sigh. She wasn't quite as excited about art as her dad – she liked things that *did* something, like baskets to put things in, or rugs to keep your feet warm. She followed her dad into the gallery and waited while Mr

Talbot chatted to the owner. Andi wandered over to the wall opposite the door and stared at some red and black and green swirls that might have been running deer, or mountains at sunset, or perhaps both.

"Sorry, Andi," her dad said, rescuing her after twenty minutes. "I got a little carried away talking to the gallery owner. Don't you love this stuff?"

"It's great," Andi said, diplomatically.

"I used to love painting back in the old days," her dad reminisced as they stepped back into the blazing sunshine. "I'm a little rusty these days but maybe I could get some lessons. I love that abstract style."

Privately, Andi thought Buddy with his paws in a can of paint could have done better. They walked along the pavement until they reached another gallery. This place had one enormous electric-blue painting hung on the wall, and nothing else.

At least Dad won't want to go in here, Andi thought. Across the road was the furniture shop she'd seen the night before with the colourful beanbags stacked in the window. They were just the thing Andi wanted for her room.

"That's beautiful!" her dad exclaimed, staring at the giant rectangle of blue. "I have to go in and ask about the artist."

"But Dad, you said we were shopping for me this morning!" Andi didn't want to sound selfish, but she couldn't face another twenty minutes of looking at pictures that didn't make much sense to her.

"I won't be long, Andi, I promise."

Andi stood in the doorway, half wishing the blue painting would fall off the wall so her dad would stop talking to the owner about it. After throwing her fifth meaningful glance at her dad (who ignored it), she decided to stop wasting her morning.

"Is it OK if I go across the road to those shops, Dad?" she called.

"Hmm?" Mr Talbot looked enquiringly at her, as if he'd forgotten she was there. "Sure, honey, go right ahead. I'll come find you."

With relief, Andi hurried out into the street. Phew! How could anyone talk for so long about something so . . . blue? Looking right, then left, she jogged across the road towards the beanbag shop, which was painted a bright bubblegum-pink.

Somewhere to her left, she heard a voice. "Sorry, fella, I didn't see you down there!"

Andi turned to see a man carefully stepping over a snoozing brown dog outside a canary-yellow shop called Santa Rosa Crafts, several doors farther down the street. With a rush of recognition, she realized the dog was the one she'd seen yesterday ambling along in the evening sunshine. She decided to go over and say hello.

"Hi, boy!" Andi felt absurdly happy to see the dog again. He seemed to remember her, because he lifted his head in greeting as she came over to stroke him. His coat was rough and flecked with grizzled white fur, and although Andi could feel his ribs as she stroked him, he wasn't worryingly thin. She gently ran her hand down his leg and picked up his paw to check underneath. His pads were tough, but not cracked like the pads of stray dogs who spent all their time on the street. It was clear he hadn't been living rough, which was a big relief.

Straightening up, Andi peered through the shop window and admired the rugs and wall hangings on display. Some beautiful woven baskets were stacked by the till, and there were several cabinets filled with carved wooden animals and glittering silver, amber and turquoise jewellery. It looked like a good place to start hunting for accessories for her room.

A tiny high-pitched sound dragged her attention away from the décor and made Andi glance round. It sounded like a kitten, but there was no sign of any cats

Santa Rose
CRAFT SHOP

in the street. Andi shook her head. Perhaps she still had water in her ears from her shower.

"I can't help it," she told the old dog, giving him one last pat. "Even though I'm on holiday, I still think like a Pet Finder!"

The door to the craft shop was open and Andi stepped inside. Wind chimes tinkled softly somewhere over her head. The shop stretched back some way, and she could see that there were more display cabinets and rails of brightly-coloured clothes at the back. The air was filled with a spicy smell, and Andi spotted a coil of incense burning in a small earthenware pot beside the till. There was no sign of a shop assistant.

There was a large rug lying beside one of the cabinets. The woven colours seemed to glow like jewels, and Andi couldn't help noticing it was the perfect size for her new room. It had a pale corn-coloured background and a black border, and in the middle there was some kind of plant – a cactus, or an abstract tree perhaps – standing in a red pot. Yellow, grey, blue and green birds flew round the branches in a whirl of activity. Andi crouched down and stroked the rug, feeling the warmth and texture of the wool. She glanced cautiously at the price tag, and whistled between her teeth. It was much more than she could afford – at least three times her Christmas money. But there was something about the rug that made it hard for Andi to tear her eyes away.

The high-pitched mewing sound came again. Andi whirled round. This time she was sure she wasn't imagining things. The mewing was much closer than it had been outside the shop. There were kittens in here! Her mind started racing. Were the kittens lost or trapped? Was their mother with them? She hadn't heard or seen any sign of an adult cat. Andi's pet-finding instincts kicked in. She started moving slowly round the shop, peering under tables and behind piles of cushions and rugs.

At last she tracked the mewing down to a beautiful red-and-gold coiled basket beside the till. Bending down, she carefully lifted the basket lid and peered inside.

"Oh, how cute!" she gasped.

There, curled in a heap of soft brown tabby fur, sat three tiny kittens.

Chapter Three

"I'm sorry, but the kittens aren't for sale."

Andi straightened up to see a girl standing beside the till. Her long black hair fell almost to her waist, and she was wearing a sea-green velveteen tunic over a pair of slim-fitting trousers with a chunky bracelet of silver and turquoise round her wrist. She looked a couple of years older than Andi.

"Are they yours?" Andi asked.

"Not exactly. We're taking care of them for a while," the girl said. She came round to Andi's side of the counter and bent down to stroke the kittens' small velvet ears.

"I heard them mewing and thought they'd got trapped or something." Andi suddenly felt rather stupid. It was clear that the girl had known the kittens were in the basket all along.

The girl smiled, making her brown eyes look warm and friendly. "Don't worry about it," she said, scooping up one of the kittens. "It's nice you were concerned. I'm Nina Nelson, by the way. My grandfather owns this shop. Are you visiting Tucson?"

"My dad lives here," Andi explained. "I arrived yesterday. My name's Andi. You've got some beautiful things," she added, looking wistfully back at the jewel-coloured rug. "Does your grandfather make the rugs?"

Nina shook her head. "Rug-making is passed from mother to daughter in Navajo tradition," she said, tucking the pale tabby kitten under her chin, where it wriggled and mewed impatiently until she distracted it by letting it play with a strand of her hair. "My mum tried to teach me lots of times, but I was always better with animals than looms!"

"I'd be hopeless at weaving," Andi confessed. "I can't even plait my friend Natalie's hair. And I'm mad about animals too!"

The girls grinned at each other. There was something about the Navajo girl that Andi immediately felt comfortable with.

The kitten under Nina's chin mewed. "Hush, Dezba," Nina murmured, stroking the kitten's soft tabby head with one finger.

"That's an unusual name," Andi ventured. "Is it Navajo?"

Nina nodded, and gently replaced Dezba in the red-and-gold basket with the others. One of Dezba's siblings reached out a paw and patted playfully at her tail. Without missing a beat, Dezba pounced on her assailant, who scrambled to the back of the basket.

"It means 'goes to war'," Nina said with a grin. "You can see she's pretty feisty!"

"What are the others called?" Andi reached into the basket and picked up a light-brown kitten with huge yellow eyes. Very carefully, she cradled the tiny creature in her hands and held it up close to her face. The kitten shook its head and sneezed, then looked rather surprised.

"That one is Nascha," Nina explained. "You see how big her eyes are? Nascha means 'owl'."

Nascha closed her eyes and gave a tiny contented purr as Andi stroked her.

"And the boy is Yas," Nina added, tickling the remaining kitten under his tabby chin. "He has splashes of white on his paws and his chest – see? Yas means 'snow'."

"I like the way their names mean something," Andi said. "I've got a dog called Buddy. I called him that because I knew straight away he was going to be my best friend."

She was about to tell Nina all about Buddy and her friends back home in Aldcliffe when a sudden pounce from Dezba tipped the basket over. It tumbled on to its side and rolled over. Sensing freedom, the kittens squeaked and clambered over one another to reach the floor. Then, with their tails stuck straight out with excitement, they tumbled off in three entirely different directions.

"If we lose them in here, we might never find them!" Nina gasped, jumping to her feet. "Quick, Andi, help me catch them!"

Andi made a grab for Yas, but he dodged behind a pile of baskets. Dezba shot beneath one of the display cabinets, while Nascha darted for the door like a small brown arrow. Nina ran to the door and slammed it shut, forcing Nascha to skid to a halt and change direction.

Lying full-length on the ground, Andi peered underneath the cabinet where Dezba was hiding. She carefully reached a hand underneath and felt around for the kitten.

"Ouch!" Pulling back, she stared at the neat line of scratches on the back of her hand. A tabby paw shot out from under the cabinet and patted a small piece of fluff before disappearing again.

"That's nothing." Nina walked over with Nascha and Yas in her arms and looked down at Andi's wounds. "It hurts much more when she bites your ankles. Once she's out, she's a real devil to catch. We could be here all day!"

"Hmm." Andi frowned. Dezba obviously had good hunting instincts. If she could find something to dangle for her, perhaps she could coax the kitten out that way. Patting her pockets for inspiration, Andi suddenly remembered the cords threaded through the hems of her combat trousers. She tugged one out until it was long enough to dangle for the kitten, and swung it lightly beside the cabinet. On cue, Dezba's paw flew after the cord, trying to snag it with her claws.

Andi moved the cord a little further away, and the paw stretched out after it. She shifted the cord a little more, and a pair of neat triangular ears appeared . . .

Pawstep by pawstep, Andi lured the kitten out of her hiding place. When Dezba had almost completely emerged from beneath the cabinet, Andi let her sink her claws into the cord, and scooped her up.

Nina whistled and looked impressed. "You must

have had a lot of practice at this kind of thing!" she said.

Andi was about to explain about the Pet Finders Club when footsteps at the back of the shop made them both look round. A tall man with white hair tied back with a leather string was walking towards them. He was dressed in dark linen trousers and a collarless white shirt with a string of amber beads round his neck. Andi moved back to make room for him and bumped into the display cabinet, making the pieces of silver, amber and turquoise jewellery shiver and tinkle.

"Please," the old man said in a low rumbling voice. "Don't look so worried. You are welcome in my shop, as long as you don't knock that cabinet over."

"She was rescuing Dezba, Grandfather," Nina explained.

Nina's grandfather frowned. "You and those cats!" he growled. "This is a shop, not a zoo! Besides, where Dezba is concerned, it is usually people who need rescuing, not the other way round. So, who is your new friend, Nina?"

"Andi, this is my grandfather, Dakota Nelson," said Nina. "Grandfather, this is Andi."

"Andi," Dakota Nelson echoed, nodding. "And what is your family, Andi?"

"Do you mean my surname?" Andi asked, surprised. "It's Talbot."

"And your mother's name?" Dakota Nelson prompted.

"Er, my mum's name was O'Keefe before she married my dad," Andi said, not sure where the conversation was leading.

Dakota Nelson seemed satisfied. "Then you are born to the clan of O'Keefe," he said. "That is how the People would see you, anyway." He smiled at Andi.

"Navajos call themselves the People," Nina explained. "I'm of the Bitter Water clan, but my grandfather is of the Deer Spring Clan. You always take the name of your mother's clan. When we meet others of the People, we always give our mother and father's clan names. That way, everyone knows exactly who you are and where you come from."

"Wow," Andi said, impressed. "That must be useful if you ever need to find someone." She thought of the times when she, Tristan and Natalie had had to hunt through phonebooks when they were pet-finding. The Navajo way would be much easier!

"So, Andi of the clan of O'Keefe," Dakota Nelson said, folding his arms. "Do you see anything that you like in my shop?"

"I love your beautiful bird rug," Andi confessed, helping Nina to put the kittens back in their basket. "But to tell the truth, I like everything in here."

"That's good to hear," Dakota Nelson said. "Sadly I don't think you are planning to buy everything, are you?"

Andi laughed. "I wish I could."

"Tell me if you want to see anything up close," said the old man, indicating the display cabinets.

"Oh, I don't want jewellery," Andi said. "I mean," she added hastily, "it's beautiful and everything, but I'm looking for things to decorate my new room."

A gasp from Nina made them look round. "Dezba's worked out how to climb out of the basket without knocking it over!" She yelped, making a grab for the scruff of Dezba's neck.

"Take those cats out back and feed them, Nina," Dakota Nelson ordered. "I am tired of having them under my feet all the time. This is—"

"A shop, not a zoo – yes, I know, Grandfather." Nina sighed as if she'd heard it a hundred times.

Andi helped carry the kittens to the back of the shop. Nina pushed through a beaded curtain and Andi followed her into a warm, cluttered kitchen.

"I don't think your grandfather likes animals very

much," she remarked, as Nina opened the fridge and took out a bowl of kitten food.

"He worries about the customers thinking that his shop is unprofessional," Nina said, setting the bowl on the floor. The kittens immediately bundled over. "But don't be fooled. I've seen him stroking the kittens when he thought I wasn't looking."

Andi played with the tip of Dezba's tail as the bossy little kitten pushed her brother and sister away from the food. "What happened to their mother?" she asked.

"She's semi-feral," Nina explained, gently pushing Yas and Nascha up to the food bowl again. "She shows up at the back gate and we give her food sometimes. I couldn't believe it when I found her with a litter of kittens! It gets really cold at night, so I brought the kittens inside. Mosi – that's what we call her, it means 'cat' in Navajo – stayed for a little while, but the desert called her back one day and she disappeared."

"She abandoned her family just like that?" Andi was shocked and sad for the kittens.

"Wild cats make their own rules," Nina said. "It's hard to accept, but it's wrong to expect them to behave the same way as domestic cats. Mosi is clever. She knows that her kittens will be safer here than out in the desert while they are so young and vulnerable."

Andi hadn't thought of it like that.

"When they're older, they can survive better in the wild because they'll be bigger and stronger," Nina continued. "It's an honour that Mosi thought we could raise her family for her, but it's hard work. She visits sometimes, but we never know when she's coming."

Andi heard her dad's voice in the shop. She pushed back the beaded curtain and waved at him. "Hello, Dad, I'm over here!" she said. "You'll never guess what I've found!"

"Trust you to find some animals on your first morning in Tucson," Mr Talbot teased when she showed him the kittens. They were curled up in a tangled heap on one of the kitchen chairs, so close it was impossible to tell where one kitten ended and another began. "They're very cute, but they aren't exactly the kind of room accessories I had in mind."

"Don't worry, Dad, they're not for sale," Andi told him.

"Perhaps they should be," Dakota Nelson grumbled from the doorway.

"Don't be mad, Grandfather," said Nina, standing

on tiptoe to kiss him on his weathered brown cheek. "Mosi will fetch them one day soon and then you won't need to worry about them any more."

"So, Andi, have you seen anything you like – apart from the kittens, I mean?" her dad asked.

Andi decided not to mention the bird rug. It was very expensive, and she didn't want to take advantage of her dad's generosity. "There are a couple of nice baskets, and I love the incense burner by the till," she said.

"Let's get those then," Mr Talbot said promptly.

Dakota Nelson rang up the purchases while Nina wrapped the incense burner in tissue paper. With her grandfather's permission, she added a free box of incense sticks – "To say thanks for catching Dezba," she explained.

"Can I come back and see the kittens again?" Andi asked.

"Come any time," Nina said enthusiastically. "Hey, do you like riding?"

Andi beamed. "I love it!"

"My mom runs a trekking centre just outside town, taking people on trail rides through the desert," Nina explained. "Would you like to come with me this weekend?"

Andi's eyes widened. Trail riding in the desert sounded fantastic! "Can I, Dad?" she begged.

"Of course you can," her dad smiled. "This is your vacation, remember. I want you to enjoy every minute."

Andi jumped in the air and gave a whoop. "Thanks, Dad! You're the best!"

Chapter Four

"Hey, watch out," Mr Talbot warned as Andi narrowly missed knocking over a pile of baskets. "You don't want to hurt yourself and not be able to ride – or decorate your room."

"What else are you doing to your room? Have you thought about painting the furniture?" Nina said, her eyes gleaming with interest.

"That's a good idea!" Andi said. "What colour should I paint everything?"

"You could try blue," Mr Talbot suggested. "It's a popular colour round here, and it would look terrific against the red floor and the white walls. We'll get some paint on the way home."

Andi glanced at the bird rug again. It would look amazing with the red tiles and the blue furniture.

Mr Nelson saw where she was looking. "That is

the tree of life," he said, leading Andi over to show her the details on the rug. "This is a cornstalk growing in a pot, with the birds of the air around it. There is a legend which says that the People were born from a cornstalk. And see this?" He pointed at a thin, pale line of wool leading to the edge of the rug's black border. "It is a spirit line. The weaver puts it in to lead her spirit back out of the rug and into the universe. Without it, many weavers believe that their spirit will remain trapped in the rug for ever."

Fascinated, Andi traced the spirit line with her finger. The rug was even more beautiful close up. She thought she recognized some of the birds – jays, and cardinals, and woodpeckers. There were butterflies and flowers and vines woven round the base of the cornstalk, and the rug seemed to glow with life.

"I love it, but I don't think I can afford it," she said honestly.

Dakota Nelson smiled. "It is still a pleasure to tell you about the pattern," he said. "I will show you more another time."

Andi put her head through the curtain to say goodbye to the kittens, and then headed outside with her dad, holding tightly on to her paper bag. Nina and her grandfather followed them, talking about the window display. The grey-muzzled dog was still sitting outside the door. Instinctively, Andi glanced back at Mr Nelson. He didn't seem to like having the kittens inside his shop. What would he say about an old dog on his doorstep?

To her surprise, Nina's grandfather came out of the shop and bent down to tickle underneath the dog's chin. He talked softly in a rhythmical language that Andi guessed was Navajo, and ran his hands down either side of the dog's neck and over his flanks. The dog squirmed with pleasure and rolled on to his back, beating his long tail against the pavement.

"This is my dog, Tate," Mr Nelson explained, standing up again. He had a gentle tone in his voice that Andi hadn't heard before. "He was a fine hunting dog in his day, but he's getting old now. These days he prefers sunbeams to rabbits, and earns his keep by bringing customers into my shop. Don't you, boy?"

Tate turned his head and gazed adoringly up at his master. Andi smiled to herself. It seemed that there was one rule for Mosi's kittens, and an entirely different one for Tate!

After calling at a hardware shop to buy a can of electric-blue paint and several brushes, Andi and her dad returned to his flat. Andi put her new baskets on the shelf above the computer, and placed the incense burner on the windowsill. Then she and her dad carried her desk, chair, bed frame and bedside table out on to the deck. Andi put on an old shirt of her dad's and set to work, painting the bed frame first because it was the biggest. Soon her hands were blue with paint from her fingertips to her wrists. The paint glowed in the bright desert light, and Andi felt a skip of excitement at the thought of the colour her furniture would bring to her little white room.

They had something to eat while the first coat was drying, and then set to work finishing it before the light faded from the sky.

"There!" Andi declared at last, leaning back to admire her handiwork. Her back ached and she was covered in blue paint, but it had been worth it. The furniture looked fantastic.

"You'll have to spend the night on your mattress on the floor," her dad advised, wiping his hands on a damp rag. "The bed frame needs to dry overnight."

"It'll feel like camping," Andi said, smiling as she remembered the conversation she'd had with her mum.

Then, as if she'd sensed Andi was thinking about

her at that very moment, her mum phoned.

"Hi, Judy," Mr Talbot said, cradling the phone under his chin. "Yes, we're doing great. Andi's right here, I'll hand you over."

"Are you OK, darling?" Judy Talbot sounded anxious on the other end of the phone. "You sounded terribly homesick in your email last night."

"I'm sorry about that, Mum," Andi apologized. "I was tired, and I really missed you and Buddy. But we've had a great time today. I found some kittens—"

"You're pet-finding already?" her mum said, astonished.

Andi laughed. "Let me finish, Mum! The kittens weren't lost. They belong to a really nice girl called Nina. Her grandfather owns this gorgeous Navajo shop. I saw the old dog from yesterday again because he belongs to Dakota – that's Nina's grandfather – and listen to this, I'm going riding in the desert at the weekend!"

"I thought you said Tucson didn't have any animals?" her mum exclaimed.

"It looks as though I found them all in one day," Andi grinned. She told her mum all about her new baskets, the tree-of-life rug and her furniture-painting.

"Well, you sound like a different person today,

Andi," her mum said, when Andi stopped for breath.

Andi moved the receiver to her other ear so she could wipe a blob of blue paint off her hand. "How's Buddy? Have you seen Natalie and Tristan?" she asked. "I've got so much to tell them."

"Buddy and I went for a long walk today," her mum said. "We met Natalie and Jet in the park. He kept sitting down in the middle of the grass and refusing to move. I think Natalie was getting a bit exasperated."

"She's been taking him to Dog Obedience classes," Andi said. "I think Jet's taking the whole sitting thing a bit too seriously. Hey, Mum, put Buddy on the phone, will you?"

She heard her mum calling Buddy and the distinctive scrabbling of the terrier's claws on the hall tiles. Suddenly she could hear Buddy's breathing, loud and clear down the line. "Bud?" she said. "Hello, boy! Are you OK without me?"

Buddy started barking so loudly that Andi had to pull the phone away from her ear. "Shush!" she protested from a safe distance. "Buddy, calm down!"

"He's going mad!" her mum warned, coming back on the line. "He can't work out where you are. OK, darling, have a good time for the rest of the week, and we'll see you soon."

"Bye, Mum." Putting down the phone, Andi felt a brief wave of homesickness wash over her. She forced her thoughts back to everything she'd done today, and felt a little better. Dezba, Nascha and Yas had been totally adorable! If she couldn't be with Buddy this week, the kittens would make great substitute pets. Plus she was still trying to furnish her new room. Where better to spend her time than the craft shop? Washing her hands at the bathroom sink, Andi decided to ring Nina and arrange to visit the Nelsons the very next day.

As soon as she was awake the following morning, Andi rushed on to the deck to check her bed frame.

"The paint has dried just enough," said her dad, joining her. "We'll move it back to your room after breakfast. We can do your chair next."

Andi wolfed down a bowl of cereal and helped carry the bed frame back into her room. Her dad had been right. The colour looked amazing against the red tiles.

"I'll get a yellow blanket to put on my bed," Andi decided. "And a yellow cushion for the chair, once we've painted that. And I'm going to get a cactus for the corner of the room today."

"Let's get a horse and a billycan for good measure," her dad joked. "And a couple of spittoons, for that authentic cowboy atmosphere. Are you going back to the Nelsons' shop today?"

"Yes, first thing," Andi said. When she'd called the previous night, Nina had invited her to help give the kittens their breakfast. "Can I borrow your camera? I want to take some photos of the kittens to send to Tristan and Natalie."

Her dad reached for his car keys. "Sure. I'll drive you over."

"Don't worry, Dad," Andi said. "I know you've got some work to do this morning. I thought I'd run, if that's OK with you." Andi spent a lot of her free time in Aldcliffe training for the school athletics team. With no Buddy to walk, no bike to ride, and her dad driving everywhere, Andi's muscles were screaming for exercise.

"Run!" Her dad sounded incredulous. "Are you sure? It must be twenty blocks."

"It's no farther than I run back home," Andi said, shrugging on a tracksuit top and tightening her trainers. "I'll phone you if I buy anything and need a lift back. What's wrong?" she added, noticing that her dad was staring at her.

"I guess I'm not used to you being so independent," he said. "I still think of you as a little kid."

"I'm ten," Andi pointed out.

"I know." Her dad smiled ruefully. "I don't know where the time's gone."

Andi kissed him goodbye, slung the camera round her shoulder, picked up a key and let herself out of the flat. The air was warm and still, with a gentle breeze. She was soon running along the pavement with her arms pumping smoothly by her sides. Her legs felt like steel springs powering her down the street, and Andi imagined that if she lifted her feet any higher, she would be flying! She arrived at Santa Rosa Crafts just as her breathing started getting a little ragged. Leaning down with her hands on her knees, Andi concentrated on getting her breath back. Tate was sitting in his usual place with his eyes closed in the bright morning light.

"Where's the fire?" Nina stood smiling in the doorway of the shop.

"No fire, just exercise," Andi panted. "Hello, Nina. How are the kittens?"

"Hungry." Nina held the door so Andi could follow her inside. "Dezba's tried to open the refrigerator already."

Mr Nelson was adding some change to the till.

"Good morning, Andi of the clan of O'Keefe," he said. "Are you taking the kittens off my hands today?"

"No, but I might buy a rug," Andi said. "Could you show me some more later on, Mr Nelson?"

"With pleasure," replied the old man. "Now hurry and feed those cats before they destroy my kitchen."

The kittens were playing a mad chasing game underneath the kitchen table. After giving them their food (and making sure Dezba didn't boss the others too much), Andi picked up Yas so she could stroke his tummy. With his deep throaty purr, Yas was fast becoming Andi's favourite – although doe-eyed Nascha and feisty Dezba were adorable as well.

"Nina!" Mr Nelson called. "Can you come out here?"

Nina and Andi went back into the shop closely followed by the kittens, who sniffed at the rugs and pounced on any loose threads they could see.

"Nina!" Dakota Nelson sighed. "Why can't you leave the kittens in the kitchen like I ask you?"

"I can't look after the shop and the kittens unless they're both in the same place, Grandfather!" Nina protested. "They'll go to sleep soon, I promise."

The wind chimes tinkled and they turned to see a middle-aged couple wearing shorts and T-shirts standing in the doorway.

"What a lovely shop," the woman said enthusiastically. She had short brown hair with streaks of grey, and a camera was slung round her neck. She turned to her husband. "Don't you think so, Jim? I could buy everything in here, I really could." She spoke with an English accent, Andi noticed.

Her husband, who wore a canvas baseball cap and white socks underneath his brown leather sandals, looked a little worried. "Not everything, Jane dear," he said. "We couldn't fit it in the camper van."

"Take a look around and let me know if I can help you with anything," Mr Nelson said with a smile. "Are those British accents, by the way?"

"That's right. We're Jim and Jane Tatford, from Hampshire in the south of England. How d'you do?" Jim Tatford shook Mr Nelson's hand and nodded at Andi and Nina.

"Are you on holiday in Arizona?" said Nina.

"Rather an extended holiday, actually," Jane Tatford said. "We've hired a camper to celebrate our retirement, and plan to tour as much of America as we can manage in the next twelve months. We started in Miami and hope to end up in Alaska."

"We're in Arizona to see Monument Valley and your famous saguaro cactuses," Mr Tatford explained.

"We're going on to the Grand Canyon in a couple of days."

Jane Tatford was looking at the tree-of-life rug. "This carpet is exquisite," she exclaimed, leaning over to get a closer look. "Look at these pretty little birds!"

Andi listened while Mr Nelson explained its significance, happy that the English woman appreciated it as much as she did.

Mrs Tatford looked round for her husband. "What do you think, Jim?"

Mr Tatford took off his hat and scratched his head. "It's lovely, but it really is too big for us, Jane," he said. "Remember, we've only just started this trip. We can't fill the camper in our first week! Why don't you choose something a bit smaller?"

Although Andi knew the rug was too expensive for her budget, she was relieved that the Tatfords weren't going to buy it. She wanted it to stay in the shop for at least as long as she was staying with her dad.

"What about this piece of pottery?" Mr Tatford said, studying a honey-coloured vase painted with a ring of stylized feathers. "This feather effect is marvellous. It's like looking at the rays of the sun."

"That's a sand painting vase," Mr Nelson explained. "Sand painting is sacred to the Navajo tradition. Our medicine men make images like this on the ground out of coloured sand – red, white, blue, yellow – to perform healing ceremonies. When the ceremony is complete, they must destroy the painting. And they must destroy it in precisely the same order in which they make it, to avoid angering the gods."

"It's beautiful," Mr Tatford murmured. "It's a salt glaze, isn't it? I wish I could get my glazes to look like that. I'm a keen potter myself – I've got a wheel in the garden shed and a kiln in the garage. I'm no painter, though. Not like the chap who made this."

After some deliberation, the Tatfords came over to the till. Mr Tatford was still holding the honey-coloured pot, and Mrs Tatford had picked up a pretty basket with a red-and-black stylized face woven into the lid. As they handed the items to Mr Nelson, Nina suddenly flew over and snatched the basket out of their hands.

"No!" she cried. "Not that one!"

Chapter Five

"What on earth—" Mr Tatford spluttered.

"Nina!" Mr Nelson growled. "What is the meaning of this disrespect to our customers?"

Nina flushed. "I'm so sorry, Grandfather; I didn't mean to be rude," she said, embarrassed. "It's just – the kittens are sleeping in this one."

Andi lifted the lid of the basket and everyone peered inside. Dezba, Yas and Nascha blinked sleepily up at them.

"Oh, aren't they heavenly!" Mrs Tatford said, reaching into the basket to stroke the kittens. "What exquisite colouring! And look at the little brown one's eyes! I've never seen anything so beautiful."

Nascha opened her mouth and gave a tiny mew. Then she snuggled back down beside her brother and sister.

Andi could see that Mr Nelson was still angry. "Nina, I told you to get rid of those cats. I can't have them disturbing the customers," he said with a frown.

Mrs Tatford looked worried. "Get rid of them? Oh no! They aren't disturbing us. In fact, they've made our day. Haven't they, Jim? We adore cats," she explained. "Our beloved Sooty died not long ago, and we miss him terribly. He had a good, long life, but nothing can replace that feeling of him curled up on my lap on a dark evening." Mrs Tatford looked sad, then brightened up again as she stroked Dezba between the ears.

"They are very pretty," Jim Tatford agreed. "Where's their mother?"

"We don't know," Nina told them. "She disappeared."

"That's awful!" Mr Tatford exclaimed. "Will she come back?"

Nina stroked Yas's tiny paws, and the little cat flexed his claws at her. "We hope so," she said. "But she's half wild. Feral cats are very unpredictable."

"We haven't seen any stray cats round here," Mrs Tatford commented.

"You don't see them very often," Nina said matter-of-factly. "They get eaten by coyotes."

The Tatfords gasped.

"Coyotes!" Andi was shocked, too. "That's horrible!"

"I know," Nina agreed. "But that's desert life for you. Oh, I'm sure Mosi, their mother, is all right," she added, seeing the expressions on their faces. "She's very wily. She's been round for a few years and knows the dangers. She'll come back, eventually."

Mrs Tatford was appalled. "But her poor kittens! What's going to happen to them?"

"They'll be fine," Nina reassured the English woman. "We can't keep them in the shop for ever, but—"

Suddenly, Dezba made a leap out of the basket. It was a long way down to the floor, but the little tabby landed neatly on her four paws and took off towards the door. Andi raced after her, reaching the door just in time to shut it. The noise from the traffic outside immediately died. Dezba narrowed her green eyes and made a dash for the window, scrambling up on to a pile of rugs by digging her claws into the wool.

"My rugs!" Mr Nelson shouted. "Those cats will ruin them!"

Dezba bunched her haunches and sprang away from Andi's outstretched hands before racing round the walls of the shop, jumping from one rail to the next in a whirl of tabby fur.

Nina put the other kittens down and hurried to help Andi. Dezba had vanished beneath a display cabinet again. This time she wasn't falling for Andi's dangling cord trick, and refused to come out.

"I hate to say it, but the other two have got out of the basket now," Mr Tatford pointed out, as Yas and Nascha tumbled happily across the floor.

Mr Nelson sighed and scooped up the wriggling kittens. Then he marched through to the back of the shop and put them in the kitchen. "When you catch Dezba, she can join the others," he told Nina and Andi, who were lying on their stomachs to peer under the cabinet. "I won't have them in my shop if they continue to make this much trouble, Nina – do you understand me? I'm sorry," he went on, turning to the Tatfords, who were waiting patiently by the till with a different basket. "Allow me to wrap those for you. Kittens never do as they are told – and neither do granddaughters."

Andi made a lightning grab underneath the cabinet. "Got you!" she declared in triumph, pulling Dezba out by the scruff of her neck. Bringing the kitten up so she was on a level with her face, Andi tapped her gently on the nose. "If you escape once more, we can't be responsible for you," she warned

Dezba. "The coyotes will get you, and that will be that!"

Dezba blinked at Andi and twitched her ears.

"She won't listen to you," Nina sighed, following Andi through to the kitchen where she placed Dezba next to her siblings in a cardboard box underneath the table.

"I know," Andi replied with a wry smile. "But there's no harm in trying."

When they came out of the kitchen, the Tatfords had gone. Mr Nelson was standing with his arms folded and a face like thunder.

Nina raised her hands. "Don't say anything, Grandfather," she begged. "I know. *This is a shop, not a zoo*. I'm sorry, and I promise it won't happen again."

Mr Nelson's expression softened. "Well," he said, "if you are truly sorry, Nina, you can help me polish the jewellery this morning."

The jewellery in the display cases was beautiful, but it was very intricate and looked difficult to clean.

"I'll help, too," Andi offered.

"Thank you." Nina's grandfather was looking less annoyed with every passing moment. "We'll start now, while the shop is quiet. Then you can play with those kittens again, if you must."

"Yes, Grandfather," Nina said humbly, but she winked at Andi to show that she knew they weren't really being punished.

They set to work with the polishing cloths, and Andi asked Nina lots of questions about the trail ride they were going to do the following day. The ponies and the scenery sounded amazing! It was great to sit there talking about trail rides while their hands were busy with the jewellery. The silver cuffs, coral and jet and agate pendants, silver belt buckles, turquoise rings and shell chokers were exquisite, and polishing them was a pleasure, not a chore. There was one beautiful necklace of silver and turquoise that Andi particularly liked, and she took extra care with each link and curve.

"That is a traditional squash blossom necklace," Nina explained. "See this curved *naja*? That means pendant, by the way." She pointed at the horseshoe-shaped pendant dangling from the bottom of the necklace. "The People learned silversmithing from the Mexicans many years ago. This pattern was based on a pomegranate flower which the Spanish settlers often wore on their clothing."

"So it's a pomegranate flower, not a squash blossom?" Andi checked, frowning.

Nina laughed. "It's both," she said. "When the style developed, the People had never seen a pomegranate, and they thought it looked like one of our native flowers, the squash blossom."

Towards the end of the morning, Andi phoned her dad to ask him for a lift home. When he came to pick her up, she towed him to the back of the shop to show him a blanket that she'd found.

"It's going to be perfect for my bed!" she said. "And guess what? It's reduced!"

"Glad to see you're being sensible about your purchases," Mr Talbot said approvingly.

Andi thought of the tree-of-life rug. It was hard to be sensible where that was concerned.

"Dad," she asked, "can Nina come back for dinner tonight? We've got stuff to plan for tomorrow's trail ride."

Mr Talbot nodded. "Sure, if it's OK with Nina's folks. It'll be a pleasure to have you, Nina." He glanced round the shop. "So where are the kittens, then? Don't tell me you've lost them, Andi. I thought you were a Pet *Finder*, not a Pet Loser."

Nina looked surprised. "Do you really find pets for people, Andi?"

"My daughter is famous for it, apparently," Mr

Talbot said with a smile. "Didn't the Queen of England call you a while back about a missing cat?"

Andi swallowed her irritation. "Very funny, Dad," she said. "I set up the Pet Finders Club with my friends Tristan and Natalie," she explained to Nina.

"That's cool!" Nina said, sounding impressed. "How many animals have you found?"

"Loads!" Andi said. "Once we found the contents of a whole pet shop."

"No wonder you were so good at getting Dezba out from under that cabinet," Nina said. "What a great idea, to set up a club to help other people who've lost pets!"

Yes, I know, Andi thought unhappily. *How come Nina understands that, but not my own dad?*

Nina agreed to come round to Andi's dad's flat at about six-thirty for dinner. Back at the flat, Andi and her dad started painting Andi's desk and chair. But the wind was picking up and dust was beginning to swirl round the deck and stick to the wet paint, so they abandoned it after a while. While her dad got them something to eat, Andi went to her room and logged on to the computer, which was sitting on the floor underneath the window. There was an email from Natalie waiting for her.

Howdy, my Arizona pal!

I'm sitting in my room wearing my scarf and thickest jumper. It's so cold here the wind burns the back of your throat, and it hasn't even snowed yet! Jet refuses to sit on my feet, even though I've tried the "sit' command lots of times. We're doing walking to heel at obedience classes now, but I can't get Jet anywhere near my feet. Most likely my new red boots are scaring him away. Have you got a tan yet?

Sprawling flat on her stomach, Andi tapped out a reply.

I'm wearing shorts and a T-shirt, ha ha! It's cold at night here and the wind is sometimes a bit gritty from the desert, but it's pretty good for January. Dad and I have been on the deck, painting my new furniture. You'd really like the colour (bright blue) and I bet you would want a tank top in the exact same shade.

I've made friends with this girl called Nina whose grandfather owns a craft shop – and she's got three kittens! They're totally adorable. Dezba's the naughty one, Nascha is the pretty

> one and Yas is just a total cutie. I'm attaching a picture that I took today with my dad's camera. They love hanging around the shop, which must seem like a big adventure playground to them – baskets to hide in, carpets to sharpen their claws on, dangling jewellery to bat with their paws. Nina's grandfather doesn't like them much though.

Andi finished off with a description of the things she had bought for her room and pressed the send button. Her email flew satisfyingly off the screen, and she smiled as she pictured Natalie reading it under layers and layers of winter clothes. Then she settled down to write to her mum and Tristan.

The wind died down in the afternoon, so Andi and her dad went back to painting the furniture. The chair was trickier than Andi thought it was going to be, and she had only just finished the second coat of paint when the light faded and she and her dad had to pack up their brushes. Andi had a long hot shower, enjoying the sensation of the water pounding on her aching muscles and washing away a tide of blue paint from her skin.

When she came out of the shower, she found Nina in the living room, talking to her dad.

"I thought we were going to have to send a search party down the drain to look for you," Mr Talbot declared. "Nina's been waiting for you to come out for the last fifteen minutes!"

"I know I'm kind of early for dinner, but I just had to come over to tell you," Nina said. "You know the trail ride we were going to do tomorrow?"

Andi looked at her in dismay. "Don't tell me it's been cancelled?"

"In a way." Nina's eyes gleamed. "My grandfather wants to take us to the Canyon de Chelly instead!"

Andi was puzzled. "Where's that?"

"It's a sacred site of the People," Nina explained. "The Navajo have lived there for hundreds of years. Very few tourists can go there, and there are parts of the canyon that you can only visit if you are with a Navajo guide. It's a three-hour drive away, so we're going to stay overnight at the canyon with some members of Grandfather's clan, who live there. It's a very special place, Andi. Your dad has already said you can come with us and I just know you're going to love it!"

Chapter Six

Andi leapt out of bed as soon as the sun peeped over the mountains the following morning. She dressed carefully – a white-and-blue check shirt, jeans and boots – and packed everything she was going to need for her overnight stay at the canyon including her dad's digital camera, which he was lending her for the trip. Last of all, she packed the dark tan leather riding chaps she'd bought back home for her riding lessons at Riverside Stables.

"Take them," her mum had advised. "They ride horses in Arizona, and knowing you and animals, you're bound to get a chance to use them." *You were so right, Mum*, Andi thought happily, zipping up her bag and cramming a red baseball cap on her head.

Her dad drove her over to Santa Rosa Crafts, where Nina and her grandfather were waiting beside an old pick-up truck that was attached to a two-horse trailer. Andi slung her bag in the back of the pick-up and scrambled into the cab beside Nina.

"Don't mind old Tate," Mr Nelson said, reaching over to pat the old hunting dog, who was sitting on the floor. "He's older than you two, so he's entitled to take up a little extra space."

Tate whined and settled his large head on Andi's knee. Andi stroked him and leant back in the worn leather seat with a sigh of satisfaction.

"We're going to pick up our horses at the trail-riding centre," Nina explained as they drove out of town. "I usually ride Raven. He's a gorgeous black quarter horse with the sweetest temper you ever saw. I think my mum will have you ride Kai. She's a dream to ride – you'll love her."

"Is Kai a Navajo name, like the kittens?" Andi asked, scratching Tate between the ears until the old dog groaned with pleasure.

"Yup, it means 'willow tree'," Nina explained. "She's a palomino, which is a kind of golden creamy colour. We can't take a horse for Grandfather because we only have a two-horse trailer, but he likes to borrow his brother's gelding, Cisco, up at the canyon."

"His brother?" Andi echoed. "So your great-uncle lives at the canyon?"

"Actually, no. Clifford's not my grandfather's brother in the American sense," Nina said. "You'd say he was a cousin. The way of the People is to call everyone 'brother' or 'sister' if you are in the same clan. If you meet people who are much older than you, then you maybe call them 'aunt', or 'grandfather'."

Andi made a face. "That sounds really confusing."

"It's easy, once you get used to it," Nina said.

Nina's mum, Angie, was waiting for them in the yard at the trekking centre. She looked just like Nina, with the same long dark hair and wide smile. She wore a velveteen blouse and faded jeans over battered suede boots, with several turquoise and coral necklaces round her neck. "I feel like I know you already," she said, giving Andi a warm hug. "Nina's been talking about you non-stop. Your pet-finding business sounds terrific."

As Nina had predicted, Angie had Raven and Kai waiting for them. Feeling that this was turning into one of the best days *ever*, Andi stroked Kai's sand-coloured nose and admired her contrasting white-blonde mane, while Nina fed Raven mints and stroked him under his whiskery chin.

"I'll look after the shop until you get back," Angie promised Nina's grandfather. "Two Clouds will take care of things here for me."

"Who is Two Clouds?" Andi asked Nina.

"He's my youngest uncle, in both the American sense and the Navajo one," Nina replied. "You'd like him – he's good fun."

"It must be great to have your family round you all the time," Andi said, a little wistfully. "I haven't got any relatives living near me, apart from my mum."

"It's OK," Nina said. "But it can get annoying sometimes. Your whole family knows everything about you – nothing is private."

Andi pondered this as they loaded the horses and said goodbye to Angie, who handed them a bag of home-made biscuits for the journey. On the whole, Andi decided it would be worth losing a bit of privacy to have such a nice family nearby.

They drove down a dusty grey road for what felt like several hundred miles, stopping off every hour to give the horses water. Tate occasionally climbed out to drink some water, but generally stayed in the cab with his head resting either on his paws or on Andi's knee.

"Tate's very quiet," Andi observed, scratching the old dog between the ears.

"He knows we're going to a sacred place," Nina said. "He's full of deep doggy thoughts. Aren't you, boy?"

Tate yawned and shifted his head slightly so that Andi could scratch him under the chin.

Nina asked her grandfather to turn on the radio, and she and Andi sang along at the top of their voices while Dakota pretended to roll his eyes at the music. At last the pick-up slowed down and turned off the main road. Andi caught her breath. Straight ahead, the flat, featureless desert reared up into the sky to form towering cliffs of bright red stone. She leant out of the pick-up truck's window to see better.

Mr Nelson pulled up beside a small ranch-house surrounded by a wooden fence. Three Navajo men were waiting by the gate.

"*Yatahey*, Clifford." Nina's grandfather climbed out of the cab and embraced a man in a big black Stetson hat. "It's been a long time, brother. How are you?"

Clifford smiled, revealing several missing teeth. "Good, Dakota. Nina, you've grown! And who is your friend?"

Nina introduced Andi to Clifford. Billy and Chee, the other men with Clifford, nodded and smiled in greeting, their silver belt buckles gleaming in the sunlight.

"My wife has prepared some lunch for us," Clifford told them. "Afterwards, Dakota will take you through the canyon to the village where you'll spend the night."

Andi and Nina helped Billy and Chee unload the horses and tie them to a rail in an open-sided barn. There was a lively paint gelding tied to the rail as well, which snorted and tossed its mane when Andi reached out a hand to stroke its velvety nose.

"That's Cisco," Nina explained. "Grandfather always rides him when we come out this way."

They followed the men into the ranch. An appetizing smell wafted out on the warm desert air and Andi's mouth watered. They'd been driving for so long; she could barely remember having breakfast.

Clifford's wife, Happy – a small woman as bright-eyed as a bird – was busily ladling out bowlfuls of lamb stew and handing them round the wooden table. Bright rugs hung on the walls, bringing flashes of colour into the room. Andi counted eight people round the table – herself, Nina, Mr Nelson, Clifford, Happy, Billy, Chee and an old woman who sat quietly in the corner with her grey hair wound up in a tight bun. She was introduced as Happy's mother, Clara.

"Why doesn't Clifford like Happy's mother?" Andi

whispered to Nina when they went outside to saddle Kai and Raven.

Nina looked surprised. "Why do you think he doesn't like her?"

"He didn't look at her once during the meal," Andi said.

Nina roared with laughter. "Don't judge what you see!" she said. "Clifford likes to keep the old ways, and it's considered taboo to look at your wife's mother."

"He never looks at her?" Andi said incredulously, tightening Kai's girth the way Shona had taught her at Riverside Stables. "But she lives in his house!"

"It's the tradition," Nina said with a shrug. She swung herself on to Raven's back and rested her feet in the stirrups. The small, powerful horse gave a snort and tossed his jet-black mane.

"Hurry up, you two," Mr Nelson said, leading Cisco out of the barn. He'd saddled the gelding so deftly that Andi had barely noticed. "Let's get going."

Andi looked back at the house. "Isn't Tate coming with us?"

"He's too old for long trips into the canyon these days," Mr Nelson replied. "Happy lit a fire, so he'll have a great time dozing in front of that. We'll see him tomorrow."

Cisco scraped the dusty ground with his front hoof. Andi admired the way Mr Nelson kept the restless horse in check, holding the reins lightly in one hand and steering the gelding with his knees. She really appreciated the lessons she'd had at Riverside, because Nina and her grandfather were obviously very experienced riders. Bending forward, she ran her hand down Kai's mane and silently asked her to take care of them both on the uneven ground. Kai jerked her head, making the bit rattle, as if she was promising to do her best.

They set off, falling into single file down a narrow path where the bright-red rock loomed high on either side. For the first time since her conversation with Tristan, Andi wondered if she'd really see a rattlesnake. A snake had frightened her pony on her first ride at Riverside, and she didn't want the same thing to happen with Kai.

When they reached a flat green plateau sliced in two by a river, Mr Nelson began to tell the legend of the Navajo.

"The People came from three different underworlds and emerged into this fourth world, the Glittering World, through a cornstalk," he began. "First Man was made in the east, from the meeting of the white and black clouds. First Woman was made in the west, from the joining of the yellow and blue clouds. They arranged our land within the protection of the four sacred mountains to the north, south, east and west. The mountains each contained the four sacred stones – abalone, coral, white shell and black jet . . ."

Andi's head filled with glittering images of gods, mountains and monsters as they left the valley and headed up towards the barren rocks. Suddenly, her attention was drawn to the cliff face. Tucked beneath a vast overhang of rock, she could see what looked like a small stone and adobe-brick village. She pointed it out to Nina.

"Is that where we're spending the night?" she asked.

Nina grinned. "Not unless you want to sleep with the spirits of the Ancient Ones," she said. "The Ancients left the canyon over seven hundred years ago, two hundred years before the People came to this place."

Andi stared at the buildings. They looked perfect, barely damaged at all, even though they had been empty for so long. "Why did they leave?"

"They ran out of water," Mr Nelson said simply. "This is a hard land, Andi."

Andi imagined the village buildings once bustling with life, and felt sad.

As they moved higher up the canyon towards the deserted village, Andi saw birds, snakes and strange dancing figures carved into the bleached rock. Most eerily of all, she saw the ghostly red outlines of handprints.

"Is this village haunted?" she asked uneasily.

Nina shook her head. "There are spirits in parts of the Canyon del Muerto, north of here," she said. "Many Navajo died there, betrayed by one of their own people during a war. It isn't place that I like to visit."

Nina's words sent shivers down Andi's spine and she urged Kai faster along the track.

The canyon grew more magnificent with each turn of the trail. Vast stacks of rock reached up into the sky like fingers, while the cliffs looked as though someone had piled up hundreds of paper-thin pancakes in every colour from palest ivory to a deep burgundy. More abandoned buildings revealed themselves around every corner, crouching under crags and overhangs of rock. They passed orchards of gnarled, stunted trees, and watered the horses at glittering creeks and waterfalls. The canyon was like a perfect, hidden world.

"I could stay out here for ever," Andi sighed, as the

setting sun made the rocks glow like molten copper. "If the weather stayed like this, I don't think I'd ever go indoors!"

"You would be in good company," Mr Nelson said. "The People believe that if they die out in the open, their spirits are free and they can dwell in the land and sky for ever."

Up ahead, Andi saw the flickering fires of a village. Unlike the abandoned village of the Ancients, this village stood away from the rocks and overhangs, and buzzed with activity. Several round mud houses with wooden doorways were scattered round a creek, smoke rising from holes set into their roofs. A camp fire blazed on a patch of open ground and the villagers were gathered around it, talking and eating.

"You've come at a lucky time," Dakota said to Andi. "The villagers usually leave the canyon in the winter time, but it's been mild enough to stay this year."

As they rode up to the village, the people got to their feet to welcome them. Three dogs came running out of one of the houses, barking furiously, and Mr Nelson knelt down and played with them until they squirmed happily in the dust by his feet. It reminded Andi of the way Nina's grandfather had been with Tate, back at Santa Rosa Crafts.

As soon as the horses were untacked and hitched to rails, bowls of food were pressed into their hands and the visitors were ushered over to the fire. Andi ate the hot meat and potato hash and beans gratefully. All this fresh air had given her an appetite to rival Tristan's!

"This is Yazzie." Mr Nelson introduced Andi to a senior-looking man who wore a red bandana round his grizzled head. Several heavy turquoise and coral rings decorated his gnarled fingers. "He's the village elder and medicine man. Yazzie's lived here all his life."

Yazzie smiled, one of his teeth glinting gold in the setting sun. His face was a map of lines and wrinkles, and his grey hair curled round his shoulders. He held Andi's gaze steadily, and Andi had a strong sense of something wise and ancient amid his thoughts. It was easy to imagine him conducting a healing ceremony with a sand painting like the one Mr Nelson had described to the Tatfords.

After supper, Andi sat wide-eyed, listening to the soothing flow of chatter, laughter and songs, and watching the flickering shadows on the mud houses and the canyon walls. Yazzie didn't speak much English, but as the fire died down and the villagers began to head to their individual houses, he beckoned Andi and Nina over to one of the huts to show them where they would be sleeping. The wooden door was so low that Andi had to duck to get through. Inside there was a pair of bunk beds piled high with red and yellow blankets. A hand loom leant against one mud wall, displaying a half-finished rug in the same coloured wool.

Andi washed her face in a bowl of water set on the floor and collapsed gratefully on her bed. Nina went to shut the wooden door.

"Oh, don't shut the door yet," Andi begged. "I can see the stars from my bunk. I've never seen them so bright."

"There is a Navajo story about the night sky," Nina said, climbing into the bunk above Andi. "In the new Glittering World, the People had arranged the mountains, the sun and the moon exactly as they wanted them. Then they tried to decide how to arrange the stars. But before they could make a decision, the Coyote – he's the trickster of many Navajo stories – came and stole the stars and scattered them at random, all across the sky."

Andi smiled as she stared up at the burning stars. They were sharp and bright as diamonds. "Random is good," she said, and closed her eyes.

* * *

In the grey light of morning, Andi, Nina and Mr Nelson saddled the horses and shook hands with the villagers, who crowded round them to say goodbye. Yazzie's hand was strong and hard like weathered oak. He smiled, and said something to Andi in Navajo.

"Yazzie says that you have a strong spirit," Nina said. She sounded impressed. "He doesn't say that about many people."

Andi felt very proud. She beamed at Yazzie, hoping he understood how pleased she was by his compliment. She really hoped she could come back to this special place one day, maybe to show her dad. As she thanked the villagers for their hospitality, she tried to fix every detail of the scene in her mind: the smell of the baked earth and the fire smoke; the colours of the villagers' clothes; the feel of their hand-woven blankets, and the warmth of their manner. She knew it was an experience she would remember for ever.

Mr Nelson led them back to Clifford and Happy's ranch by a different route, high above the rushing river. The views were breathtaking, stretching far across the canyon with the river running like a thin brown thread below. Andi felt as if they were journeying forward through time, returning to the modern world which had seemed so far away in the Navajo village.

Back at the ranch, Tate thumped his tail on the hearth rug in greeting.

"He hasn't moved from the hearth since you left," Happy told them.

"Very sensible, at his age," Mr Nelson said, as Tate slowly got to his paws and walked across the room to press his nose into his master's hand. "You missed nothing you haven't seen before, old friend."

They loaded the horses into the trailer and stowed their bags, then said goodbye to Clifford and his family. Andi rested her hands on the back of the seat, watching through the rear window as the great cliffs of the Canyon de Chelly faded into the distance. She couldn't wait to upload the pictures she'd taken on her dad's camera, and she decided that if any of the pictures were good enough she was going to get them enlarged and framed to hang on the walls of her new room.

They took Kai and Raven back to the trail-riding centre, where Andi met Nina's uncle, Two Clouds. He was eager to hear about their trip, and it was obvious he felt a strong connection to the place where his ancestors had lived for hundreds of years. Then they piled into the pick-up again and headed back to Santa Rosa Crafts.

"We're back!" Mr Nelson called, putting the bags down by the till. "Angie, are you here?"

Andi looked round for the kittens. She was dying to pick them up and cuddle them.

Nina was obviously feeling the same way. "Mum?" she asked, as Angie came out of the kitchen drying her hands. "Where are the kittens?"

"Welcome back, you two," Angie smiled. "I haven't seen the kittens since lunch. They're probably asleep somewhere."

Nina paused. "Since lunch?" she echoed. "But it's five o'clock, Mum. Are you saying that you haven't seen them all afternoon?"

Angie frowned. "No. Should I have?"

"Didn't you feed them at three?" Nina was beginning to look anxious.

"I put out their food, yes," Angie said. Now she was looking worried too.

Nina hurried to the kitchen and checked the food bowls. Then she turned round and stared in horror at Andi. "Their food is still there," she said. "They always eat it – every last scrap. I think . . . I think they've disappeared!"

Chapter Seven

"Disappeared?" Andi gasped. Finding animals in Aldcliffe was one thing, but Tucson . . . It was more than three times the size, for a start, and she barely knew ten roads there. And the kittens were so tiny! Thoughts of hungry coyotes loomed terrifyingly in her mind.

"Andi, you're good at finding pets." Nina grasped Andi's arm. "What should we do?"

Andi pulled herself together. Her pet-finding instincts were already kicking in. First, they needed to pinpoint exactly when the kittens disappeared. Suddenly she wasn't tired any more. She hunted in her bag for a pen and paper. *If Tristan were here,* she thought ruefully, *he'd have one of his red notebooks for keeping track of the investigation*. But the other Pet Finders were hundreds of miles away, and Andi was on her own.

"Mrs Nelson," she said in her calmest, most professional voice. "Please think back. When is the last time you're sure that you saw the kittens?"

"Just before lunch, I think," Angie said, frowning. "Yes – they went to sleep in one of the baskets at around one o'clock. I remember noticing when I went out back to grab something to eat."

"Could they have gotten out of the door when you weren't looking?" Mr Nelson asked.

Angie shook her head. "I kept the door closed all day because the wind kept blowing dust into the shop. I spent half the afternoon sweeping the floor and shaking the rugs."

Andi made a note. "What about when the customers came in and out? You said the shop was busy today."

"You mean they could have got out when a customer came in?" Angie looked worried. "Would they really go out in the street on their own?"

"They have been getting more adventurous," Nina said, white with anxiety. "Especially Dezba. If she got outside, the others would have followed her."

"Oh, this is awful!" Angie was close to tears. "You leave me in charge for one day and this happens. Nina, I'm so sorry."

Nina patted her mum on the shoulder. "It's OK," she said. "Andi finds pets back home all the time. She's practically a professional."

Andi smiled at Nina. "Thanks for the vote of confidence," she said, trying not to let her anxiety show in her voice. "Firstly, let's do a really thorough search of the shop. If they're still inside, that'll be the quickest way to find them."

Angie Nelson and Nina's grandfather went to look upstairs while Andi and Nina turned the sign on the door to *Closed* and searched every inch of the shop, looking underneath each cabinet, turning all the baskets and pots upside down and peering inside every rolled-up carpet. Andi went through the stock in the window as well, and Nina emptied the cupboards in the kitchen. They hunted in drawers, behind wall hangings – they even opened the jewellery cabinets. But the kittens were nowhere to be found.

"Well, this is a hive of industry." Mr Talbot stood in the doorway gazing at Andi and Nina, who were on their knees among piles of baskets, rugs and pots. "I came to take you home, Andi, but it looks like you're pretty busy. Did you have a good trip?"

"Dad!" Andi scrambled to her feet and ran over to

him. "The trip was fantastic, but I'll tell you about that later. The kittens have disappeared! Can you close the door behind you? Just in case the kittens are in here somewhere and get out."

Mr Talbot looked taken aback. "Yes, ma'am," he said, shutting the door. "Do you want to search me as well?" He pulled his pockets inside out and held his arms out to the side.

Andi felt impatient. "Dad, this is no joke. Help us look, will you?"

"Of course," her dad said hastily. "Where shall I start?"

"We've covered pretty much everywhere except the top shelves over there," Andi said, pointing. "Even with the stepladder, Nina and I aren't tall enough to search them. You're tall, Dad – can you reach them?"

Mr Talbot pulled a stepladder towards him and climbed up to examine the shelves. "You seem to know what you're doing," he remarked, hunting through the neatly-stacked baskets. "I wouldn't have thought of looking up here."

"I've had a lot of practice finding pets, remember?" Andi said. She waited for her dad to come back with one of his joking replies. But he just nodded, and turned to the next stack of baskets.

They continued hunting for another hour, carefully searching their designated areas, but finding nothing.

"Anything upstairs?" Nina demanded when Angie Nelson and Nina's grandfather returned.

Mr Nelson shook his head. "Nothing," he said heavily. For all his complaints about the kittens in the shop, it looked as though deep down he was as fond of them as Nina and Andi were.

Andi looked round for Tate. The old hunting dog was sleeping on a blanket at the back of the shop. "If we gave Tate one of the baskets the kittens used to sleep in, do you think he'd be able to use his nose to help us find them?"

Mr Nelson looked uncertain. "His sense of smell isn't what it used to be, but we can give it a try," he said. "Tate, boy, come!"

Tate heaved himself to his paws and padded over. Mr Nelson showed him the red-and-gold basket Andi remembered seeing the kittens in the very first time she visited the shop. Tate sniffed at it, blinked up at Mr Nelson, and then ambled back to his blanket, where he collapsed with a sigh.

Mr Nelson shrugged apologetically. "I guess he's not a hunter any more," he said. "I did warn you."

Andi stifled a yawn, suddenly feeling dog-tired herself.

"Listen," Mr Talbot said, checking his watch. "It's getting pretty late and you've had a long day. We should call it a night."

"But, Dad—" Andi started to protest.

"No, Andi," said her dad, sounding firm. "I know from experience that you can't do a good job when you can't keep your eyes open."

"The same goes for you, Nina," Angie Nelson said gently. "We've done the best we can tonight. We will keep looking in the morning."

Nina's eyes filled with tears. "But the kittens are too young to be out on their own without their mum all night!"

Mr Nelson put his arm round Nina's shoulders. "Dezba will keep them all together," he said. "She's got the makings of a fierce little mother herself. Don't worry, Nina. Everything will be OK."

As soon as they got back to her dad's flat, Andi logged on to the computer and sent an email to Tristan and Natalie. They might have been hundreds of miles away, but she needed their help.

SOS!
The kittens are missing! We've searched the shop and the flat upstairs, but there's no sign of them.

She tapped out a few more details about the shop and sent the email. Then she sat and stared at the blank screen, gnawing at her thumbnail while she waited hopefully for a reply. There was no response. It looked as though Natalie and Tristan weren't online just then. Sighing, Andi got ready for bed. Sleep took a long time to come.

The first finger of light had barely peeped through the curtains before Andi was back sitting at her computer. There were two responses waiting for her.

Andi – sorry about the kittens. Have you tried the local animal shelter? Someone may have found them and handed them in. If the three of them stuck together like you think, they would have been pretty noticeable out on the street. And I don't want to worry you, but Tucson is major snake country and the kittens could end up as reptile food if you don't find them soon.
See you (wouldn't want to be you)
Tristan

"Great," Andi muttered to herself. "First coyotes, now snakes." Trying not to think about all the dangers lurking in the desert, she jotted down Tristan's idea about the shelter. She'd have a look in her dad's phonebooks as soon as she'd read Natalie's email.

> Hi Andi, Nat here! Listen – I checked your last email and you mentioned how you first saw the kittens in a basket in the shop. I wondered if maybe someone could have bought a basket containing the kittens by mistake? It's probably a daft idea, but worth thinking about perhaps.

Andi stared at the screen. "Nat, you're a *genius*!" Nina's mum had said that the kittens fell asleep in a basket just before lunch. They could easily have stayed asleep most of the afternoon – and someone could just as easily have bought them. Nina's mum had been very busy yesterday. She might have forgotten to check the baskets she was selling. That English couple had almost bought a basket containing the kittens the other day, now Andi came to think of it.

She pulled on some clothes and ran into the living area. "Dad!" she called. "Can you give me a lift to Santa Rosa Crafts, *now*?"

Her dad appeared at the bathroom door, his face

half covered with shaving foam. "Let me shave first," he protested, waving his razor. "I can't show up to work with half a moustache."

Andi waited impatiently for her dad to finish, then dashed into the bathroom to clean her teeth and splash some cold water on her face. She pulled on her trainers and grabbed her bag and her dad's camera with one hand and a piece of toast with the other.

"Go as fast as you can, Dad," she begged, as Mr Talbot steered his Jeep out on to the road heading into town.

They reached Santa Rosa Crafts ten minutes later. Barely stopping to wave goodbye to her dad, Andi sprinted into the shop and looked round. "Nina!" she called. "Mr Nelson? Mrs Nelson? Anyone here?"

Nina pushed through the beaded curtain at the back of the shop. She had a box of cat food in her hand and she looked as if she hadn't slept all night.

Andi looked at the food. Hope soared in her heart. "Have you found them? Where are they? Are you giving them breakfast?"

"No, I don't know, and no again," Nina said wearily. "I've been out since dawn, shaking this box. They usually come running when they hear it, you see. But not this time. Oh, Andi, what are we going to do?"

"Listen," Andi said urgently. "My friend Natalie's had a great idea . . ." She told Nina what Nat had suggested about the baskets.

Nina went pale. "But if they were sold in a basket, we'll *never* find them!"

"We will if your mum kept a record of what she sold yesterday," Andi assured her. "We can trace people that way. Perhaps your mum can remember which basket she saw the kittens sleeping in?"

"I'm sorry, but I can't remember," Angie Nelson said, overhearing them. "But I do remember selling a couple of baskets yesterday. I can check the receipts."

"Good," Andi said. "I've got a back-up plan as well. My friend Tristan suggested that we should visit the local animal shelter. I should have thought of that straight away. Is there a shelter nearby?"

"The nearest one's a couple of streets away," Nina told her. "Mum, can we head over there right now?"

"Sure," Angie Nelson agreed. She was already checking through the previous day's receipts, which she had taken out of the till. "Maybe I'll have some information for you by the time you get back."

Andi and Nina ran all the way to the shelter, which was tucked down a dusty side street and had cheerful, sun-faded posters of dogs and cats pinned up in the windows. Inside, Andi saw a wall of kennels containing lost and stray animals to one side of the reception desk. There were several skinny dogs like Tate; a cockatoo with a pale pink crest and a missing claw; three iguanas that were sitting motionless underneath a heater. But there were no cats to be seen. Andi couldn't help thinking nervously of coyotes again.

Ahyoka, the woman behind the reception desk, listened carefully as Andi explained what had happened. But to Andi's dismay, she shook her head.

"I wish I could tell you something different, but no one brought in any kittens yesterday," she said apologetically.

Nina's shoulders sagged. "OK," she said. "It was worth a shot. Are there any other animal shelters in town that might be worth checking out?"

"There are several, but they're all a couple of miles away," said Ahyoka.

The kittens were unlikely to have travelled that far. Andi glanced at the notice board, which was dotted with posters of missing animals. They reminded her of all the posters she'd made with the Pet Finders Club back home.

Ahyoka saw her looking. "If you have a photograph of the kittens, you could put together a poster on the shelter computer," she suggested. "I don't mind printing off a few copies for you."

"We don't have any photos," Nina began, but Andi grabbed her arm.

"I've got my dad's camera!" she said. A piece of good luck at last! "I took some pictures of the kittens a couple of days ago, remember?"

Ahyoka showed them how to use the computer. It wasn't very different from Andi's mum's computer back home, and Andi was soon uploading photos and designing text.

"You make this look so easy," Nina said, watching Andi type in the Santa Rosa Crafts phone number. "I'm so glad you're here, Andi. I just wish I didn't have to use your pet-finding experience, if you know what I mean."

She sounded so sad that Andi reached over and squeezed her hand. "We're doing everything we can," she promised. "I'm the expert, remember? We'll find them; I'm sure of it."

She smiled encouragingly at Nina, who managed a watery smile in response.

After taking down a detailed description of the

kittens, Ahyoka made a note of Nina's phone number. "This really isn't the best place for kittens to get lost in. I heard a pair of coyotes in my back yard last night, howling away. But if they stick together they might be OK," she added, handing a stack of the freshly-printed posters to Andi, who pinned one up on the notice board and put the rest in her bag. "I promise I'll call at once if I hear anything."

"We can't thank you enough for your help," Nina said.

Ahyoka looked a little sad. "I just hope that you find them soon," she said.

Her meaning was clear.

Before the coyotes do.

Chapter Eight

Nina had obviously picked up on Ahyoka's concern too. She was very quiet as they walked back to Santa Rosa Crafts.

"Perhaps your mum has traced some of yesterday's customers," Andi said, trying to cheer them both up.

"Maybe," Nina said gloomily. "But most of our customers are tourists. Even if Mum finds some names, they might already have left town."

"We have to think positive," Andi urged. "It's one of the first rules of pet-finding. We've had some cases back home that looked totally hopeless, but they turned out OK in the end."

Nina looked a little happier. "As hopeless as this one?"

"Worse," Andi assured her. "We had to deal with a flash flood once when we were out looking for a missing pony! And when more than twenty animals went missing from our local pet shop, it took ages to find just *one*! Look, there's your mum. Let's see what she's found out."

Angie Nelson had good news. "I have four names for you," she said triumphantly, waving a list at them.

Nina looked at the receipts. "The first three are for baskets that don't have lids, Mum," she said sadly. "The kittens could only have left the shop without anyone knowing if the basket had a lid."

"Oh, I didn't think of that." Angie took back the receipts and the list with a frown.

"One name is a start," Andi said, determined to stay positive. She looked at the receipt. "It looks as though this customer bought several baskets. That should help our chances!" She read the name on Angie's list. "Helena Miller. Is this a local address?"

"Helena's one of our regular customers," Mrs Nelson explained. "She's a beautician, and her salon is only two or three streets away from here. Listen, I have to head back to the trekking centre now, but call me if anything comes up, OK?"

Andi and Nina nodded, then sprinted for the door. This was definitely a lead worth following up!

* * *

Helena Miller's beauty salon had a bright red-and-green awning, rows of hairdryers lined up along the back wall, a nail bar by the window, and framed black-and-white photographs of film stars on the walls.

"Those look as though they came from your shop," Andi said, pointing to a display of red and green baskets in the window.

The baskets had been filled with snowy white tissue paper, bottles of body lotion and small packets of soap tied with red and green ribbons. The lids lay decoratively beside each basket.

Nina stood on tiptoe to peer into the display. "There's no sign of any kittens in those," she said.

"Perhaps she bought some more baskets that she hasn't used yet," Andi suggested. She pushed open the door and led the way into the parlour's cool interior. "Hello? Miss Miller?"

A tall woman with blonde hair pinned neatly on top of her head looked up from the reception desk. "Can I help you?" she asked, smiling. "Oh, hello, Nina! How's your mom?"

"Fine thanks, Miss Miller," Nina said. "We're looking for some lost kittens, and wondered if we could ask you about the baskets you bought yesterday."

Nina explained how they thought the kittens

might have been sold inside a basket by mistake. As Nina was talking, Andi took out one of the posters from her rucksack.

"How adorable!" the beautician exclaimed. "I'm sorry, but my baskets were empty. You can see them in the window there." She indicated the display.

"Are you sure that when you took off the basket lids, the kittens weren't inside?" Andi checked. "They're very good at escaping when no one's looking."

Miss Miller shook her head. "I would have noticed," she said. "And even if I hadn't, one of my customers certainly would have."

Andi rolled up the poster and began putting it back into her bag. But Miss Miller held out one of her elegantly-manicured hands. "I'll put that in the shop window if you like," she offered. "It's the least I can do."

"Thanks," Andi said gratefully, pushing the poster back across the desk.

"Do you have any more leads?" Miss Miller asked.

"It's kind of hard to trace everyone who bought baskets yesterday," Nina admitted sadly. "Mum says there were lots of other customers, but they were tourists and they paid in cash."

Miss Miller drummed her fingers on her desk.

"Have you tried the local motels, or the campsite on the edge of town?" she suggested. "That's where most of the tourists stay."

"Thanks, that's a really good idea!" Nina said. "My cousin Olivia works at the Sunny Inn. She might be able to help us."

"And if she can't, we can at least put up a few posters," Andi put in. She suddenly felt really grateful for all the help they were getting from the Tucson locals. Even though the city was much bigger than Aldcliffe, there was a real feeling of community spirit in Nina's district, and enthusiasm about finding the missing pets. "Thanks, Miss Miller. You've been a real help!"

It was a brisk fifteen-minute walk to the Sunny Inn on the edge of town. Nina and Andi walked down several residential roads, across a children's playground, and past a row of small shops and a couple of warehouses. Soon they could see the Sunny Inn's cheerful neon sign.

"Nina!" the girl on the reception desk greeted them. She had a cute heart-shaped face and sparkling green eyes behind stylish tortoiseshell glasses. "Great to see you! To what do I owe this pleasure?"

"It's no pleasure, Olivia," Nina said glumly, after

introducing Andi. She showed her cousin one of the posters. "We're looking for Mosi's kittens."

Olivia's face fell. "Those cute little things have gone missing?" she said in dismay. "But they're really tiny and so helpless!"

To Andi's surprise, Nina's cousin looked close to tears. Nina glanced at Andi. "Olivia's kind of emotional," she whispered apologetically. "Listen, Ol, it's not over yet. They're semi-feral, remember? They've got a better chance than most domesticated kittens would have."

Nina's cousin sniffed and reached for a tissue. "Sorry," she gulped. "It's just – they're so cute and very small . . . Oh dear . . ."

"Can we put up a poster?" Andi put in, before Olivia started bawling.

Olivia wiped her eyes and reached for the poster. "You think they were sold in a *basket*?" she said in surprise, after reading the text. "Well, there's a guest at the motel who came in with a Santa Rosa Crafts bag yesterday afternoon."

"Are they still staying here?" Andi queried, suddenly feeling hopeful. "Could we speak to them?"

Olivia pinned the poster on the notice board behind the desk. "She's in room 305," she said, reaching for another tissue and blowing her nose. "Listen, I really hope you find them. Call me when you do, OK?"

Nina and Andi hurried across the car park to room 305, and Andi knocked tentatively on the door. It was opened by a young woman with cropped blonde hair and a friendly smile. An untidy rucksack stood by the door, packed close to bursting.

"I remember those kittens," she said, studying the poster. "They were curled up in a basket by the cash register."

"What time was that?" Andi asked.

"It was three-thirty," the blonde woman said promptly. "I noticed a shop right across the street with a large clock in the window. You know, Santa Rosa Crafts is such a great little place!" she enthused. "I bought this cute bear." She showed Andi and Nina the carved stone bear, which held a miniature fish in its paws. "The white bear is a powerful healing object, perfect for my brother, who has problems with his back." She also showed them a tiny earthenware pot painted with an image of the moon. But it was so tiny that even Dezba's paw wouldn't have fitted inside. "I have to buy small," she said, nodding at her bulging rucksack. "I loved all the stuff at the shop, but I didn't have space for anything bigger."

"Another dead end," Nina sighed as they headed for the local campsite. "Is pet-finding always like this?"

"But, Nina, we've actually got some important information," Andi pointed out. "Remember what that woman said about noticing the clock across the street? If we can work out exactly *when* the kittens disappeared, we're more likely to find them."

"I suppose," Nina said, sounding unconvinced. "Come on, we may as well check out the campsite. It's not far from here."

She led the way down a path fringed with long yellow grasses, dotted with tiny flowers. Andi ran her hand along the furry tops of the grasses, enjoying the tickling feeling on her fingers.

Nina stopped so suddenly that Andi almost bumped into her. "Listen," she hissed. "Can you hear something?"

Something was rustling in the grass beside the path. Andi hunkered down and peered into the verge. "There aren't any snakes around here, are there?"

Nina shrugged. "Some," she said. "But they don't rustle so loud."

Was it possible that the kittens had escaped from

the campsite and were making their way home along the path? Andi shuffled forward, listening intently. Then—

"Oh!" She scrambled to her feet as something resembling a very small pig came hurtling out of the grass towards them. "What's *that?*"

The hairy little creature cocked its ears and stared hard at Andi and Nina. The sunlight gleamed on its rough grey coat and a pair of very small, very sharp-looking tusks.

"It's a javelina," Nina said, grinning at the expression on Andi's face. "It means 'little spear' in Spanish."

"Because of its tusks, right?" Now she'd got over her fright, Andi was fascinated. She wrinkled her nose. "It's pretty smelly. What is it, some kind of wild pig?"

Nina shook her head. "Actually, it's not related to the pig family at all," she said. "It's something to do with having a different number of toes, and the way its tusks point down instead of up."

"Weird," Andi murmured. Now she took a closer look at the javelina, she could see that it had a longer, finer snout than a pig. There was a collar of pale fur round its neck, and it had little black legs and hooves.

The javelina had clearly decided the girls weren't a threat. It turned to the nearest prickly pear and took a

bite out of a long fleshy leaf covered with ferocious spikes, chewing it as though it was a marshmallow.

"I don't fancy the kittens' chances if they bump into one of them," Andi remarked, looking at the javelina's sharp teeth and tusks.

"Don't worry; it's a vegetarian," Nina assured her. "They're pretty common around here. I guess they're cute in a way, but I wouldn't have one as a pet."

After one last suspicious glance at Andi and Nina, the javelina shuffled into the undergrowth and disappeared.

The campsite manager was a clean-shaven young man with his hair pulled back in a slick black ponytail. He hadn't seen the kittens, but he took three posters and promised to put them up around the site that afternoon. Glancing round the little white reception caravan with its view across the camper vans and brightly-coloured tents of the campsite, Andi suddenly thought of the English couple with their camper van who'd come into the shop three days earlier. They had mentioned that they were staying at the local campsite. Andi knew they'd want to hear about the kittens.

"The Tatfords?" the manager echoed when Andi

asked about them. "British, right? We don't get too many British here." He leant his arms on the desk. "They headed for the Grand Canyon last night. I think they were planning on taking it easy and stopping off along the way. Tourists love that highway route. There's plenty to see. We were sorry to see them go. They were real nice people."

"Yes, they were," Nina agreed. "Oh well, please can we ask around the campsite in case any of your guests were in my grandfather's shop yesterday?"

"Sure you can," said the man. "Good luck."

Nina knocked on the doors of the caravans and the camper vans, while Andi checked the tents. But there weren't many people about, and although the few tourists they met took an interest in the posters, they weren't able to help.

"Most people are probably out shopping," Nina guessed.

"Or hiking, or doing some other holiday-type things," Andi agreed.

They walked despondently towards the gates. A tourist in a large floral shirt and straw hat was coming out of the reception building ahead of them, carrying a shiny galvanized bucket.

"Excuse me, but were you in Santa Rosa Crafts

yesterday?" Andi tried. "We're looking for three missing kittens."

The tourist took off his hat and scratched his thinning hair. "I've never heard of that shop, but – come to think of it – I did see a kitten today. Where was it now?"

Andi's eyes widened. She looked at Nina.

"I walked into town first thing," the tourist said slowly, backtracking through his day. "I got a coffee at that diner place – no, it wasn't there, they had a dog . . ."

Come on! Andi begged silently.

"I remember!" he said at last. "The hardware shop where I picked up this bucket! The guy there definitely had a kitten!"

Chapter Nine

"Was it tabby or brown – like the kittens in the poster?" Andi checked.

The tourist studied the poster. "Yeah, kind of like that," he said.

"What was the name of the hardware shop?" Nina prompted.

"Hudspith, or Hudson, or something like that," the tourist said.

"Hobson?" Nina suggested.

"That was it!" the tourist agreed. "Now, if you don't mind, I've gotta go fix my water tank. Good luck with your search." He brandished the bucket at them in farewell and strode into the campsite.

"Hobson's is only one street away from Santa Rosa Crafts!" Nina exclaimed. "You can reach it down the alley at the back of our shop. The kittens could have escaped and made it to the hardware shop on their own, or maybe Mr Hobson found them in the alley. Come on, let's go check it out!"

"The man said there was only one kitten," Andi warned, following Nina back down the path where they saw the javelina.

"He only *saw* one kitten," Nina corrected her. "The other two could have been hiding. Hardware shops are like our shop – the kittens could find hundreds of hiding places!"

"That's true," Andi said. She didn't like to tell Nina that the other two could be somewhere completely different. And if they had split up, the job of finding them was going to be three times harder.

"Come on!" Nina insisted, breaking into a run. Andi ran alongside her, glancing at the undergrowth in case the javelina put in another appearance. It had been cute, and unlike any wild creature she had seen before. But the long grass was silent.

They ran side by side all the way back into town. Andi enjoyed feeling the sun on her shoulders as she jogged along the dusty pavement. The first thing she noticed back at the shop was that Tate wasn't in his usual sunny spot. She'd got used to seeing the old hunting dog lying underneath the shop window with his eyes closed. The shop front seemed oddly empty without him.

"Where's Tate, Mr Nelson?" she asked, as she and Nina headed for the kitchen and a long, cool drink of water.

Mr Nelson was locking one of the jewellery cabinets. He took out the key and weighed it thoughtfully in one hand. His expression was unreadable. "That is an interesting question," he said. "And I'm afraid that I don't have an answer. He went for a walk this morning but he hasn't come back yet."

"You mean Tate's gone missing too?" Nina gasped. "No! He can't be. Not now, with the kittens and everything – he just *can't*!"

To Andi's dismay, she covered her eyes and burst into tears. Andi waited for Mr Nelson to tell them that Tate wasn't missing, that he'd probably just gone for a wander, but to her surprise he didn't. Instead, he put his arms round Nina and held her close. His eyes were dark and strangely serene, as though he knew there was more meaning to Tate's absence than just going for a walk. Andi felt a lump in her throat, and she clenched her jaw to stop the tears from breaking through.

Nina sniffed. "Sorry," she gulped. "It's just – on top of losing the kittens, it seems so unfair."

Andi had a sudden, horrible thought. "What if Tate's been hit by a car or something?"

"Tate's a wise old dog," Mr Nelson murmured. "He'll take care of himself."

"Don't you *care* about Tate?" Nina said, sounding angry. "He could be hurt! How can you just stand there and—"

Mr Nelson held up his hand. "Enough."

"Enough?" Nina looked appalled. "Tate's your dog, Grandfather! How can you be so calm?"

Andi opened her mouth to make some suggestions about finding dogs. But there was a look in Mr Nelson's eyes that stopped her. He did care about Tate – she knew he did. Perhaps he just wasn't ready to talk about him yet. She'd seen other pet owners in denial when their pets first went missing.

"Tell me, Nina," Mr Nelson said firmly. "What have you and Andi been doing today?"

Andi knew they had to respect Mr Nelson's feelings if he didn't want to talk about Tate.

"Someone saw a kitten in Hobson's today," Nina sniffed, wiping her eyes. "We thought we'd go check it out." Her lip trembled again. "But what if it's not the right kitten? I don't think I can take any more bad news today."

"Good or bad, we've got to find out," Andi told her. "It's another piece of the puzzle. You can't see the picture until the jigsaw puzzle is finished, and every piece plays a part in the end."

Nina gave a sad smile. "I guess you're right," she said.

Mr Nelson fetched two glasses of water for them. He didn't say anything else about Tate, and Andi wondered if he was being sensitive, trying not to upset Nina with another missing pet. She guessed he must be feeling anxious inside, knowing how fond he was of the old hunting dog. Or perhaps he thought Tate would come wandering back in his own time.

When they were feeling less thirsty and a little calmer, Andi and Nina set off along the alley that led to Hobson's hardware shop. The alley wound uphill until Andi was treated to a view of the whole of Tucson, spreading as far as the distant dusty mountains surrounding the city. Although Nina's district had a cosy villagey feel to it, the view reminded Andi of just how big the whole of the city of Tucson was in comparison to Aldcliffe. She tried not to think about how much harder it was going to be to find the missing animals in a place this size.

Hobson's stood at the end of the alley, its dark-blue

shop front neatly painted. Brushes, plastic buckets, boxes of nails and bolts and screws, and a faded sign about fireworks were displayed in the window.

Nina glanced at Andi. "Think positive, right?" she said, biting her lip.

"Right," Andi said, and gave her an encouraging high-five.

They walked together into the dim, dusty interior. The shop owner was sitting by the till with his feet on the desk and his nose deep in the sport pages of the local newspaper.

"Hi, Mr Hobson," said Nina.

The shop owner swung his feet to the floor. "Hi, Nina," he said, giving Andi a friendly nod. "Not with your grandfather today?"

Nina shook her head. "I know this sounds kind of strange, Mr Hobson," she began, "but can we see your kitten?"

Mr Hobson looked puzzled. "My kitten? She only just arrived. How come you know about her?"

"Someone told us they'd seen her," Nina said.

Andi gave her best smile. "We're mad about animals," she gushed. "I hear your kitten is the cutest thing ever. Please may we see her? We won't stay too long."

"Well, sure. If you want to," Mr Hobson said with a shrug. "Come on back."

He walked to the back of the shop and pushed aside the curtain separating the shop front from his living room. "She's right there," he said, pointing to a large green chair by the window. A fluffy grey kitten sat up and looked at them with her head on one side.

"Oh no!" Nina groaned. She sat heavily on the edge of the armchair and put her hands over her eyes. "It's the wrong kitten!"

"Is Nina OK?" Mr Hobson asked Andi.

"She's just disappointed," Andi told him, feeling sick with disappointment as well. "She's lost three kittens, you see, and we're trying to find them."

"That's too bad," Mr Hobson said sympathetically. "Smokestack here came from a friend downtown – she was the last one in the litter. But, you know, I did hear of someone else recently who'd got some new kittens. Now who was it . . .?"

Nina lifted her head.

"Please try to remember," Andi said. "It could be really important."

Mr Hobson thought hard. "Got it!" he exclaimed. "Dave – he works here Saturdays – told me that he

served a couple who asked him where the pet shop was, because they'd just got some kittens."

Andi looked at him. "Kittens, with an 's'?" she checked, just to be sure.

Mr Hobson nodded. "I'm pretty sure that's what Dave said."

"Brilliant!" Andi said, smiling at the shop owner. She could tell he was still worried about Nina, who was staring out of the window. "Where's the pet shop?"

"Oh, not far." The shop owner pointed down the street. "Nina knows where it is, she'll show you."

After thanking Mr Hobson several more times, Andi towed Nina outside. "This is a really good lead," she said, squeezing Nina's arm. "It's the first mention we've had of more than one kitten!"

Nina shrugged. "If you say so."

Andi could tell that all the dead ends were beginning to get Nina down. "Pet-finding is *always* like this," she explained. "If that tourist hadn't told us about the man in the hardware shop, we wouldn't have picked up this new clue. We'll find Mosi's kittens soon, I know it! And then we'll start looking for Tate."

Nina didn't look convinced. "The pet shop's this way," she said gloomily. "Come on."

A delivery lorry was parked outside the shop with

its back doors open. A young man in a blue T-shirt printed with the silhouette of a dog and the words *Pets4Ever* – the name of the shop – was unloading boxes of food, pet beds and what looked like the frame of a new aquarium on to the pavement.

"He must work here," Andi said, nudging Nina. "Look at his T-shirt. Er, excuse me." She followed the man through the door, Nina close behind her.

"Not now, kid," Blue T-shirt said, dumping an armful of boxes on the floor. "I'm busy."

"It won't take a minute," Andi insisted, following him back outside. "Do you remember someone coming into the shop yesterday to buy things for some kittens?"

Blue T-shirt had disappeared back inside the lorry. Andi and Nina waited patiently until he jumped back down with another box in his arms. It looked heavy.

"Perhaps we should help him unload," Nina suggested.

Andi nodded. "Good plan. Do you want a hand?" she offered, taking one side of the box before Blue T-shirt could protest.

"I'll bring in some of these pet beds." Nina reached into the lorry and piled up several of the beds until they wobbled alarmingly in her arms. "We really need to talk to you, sir."

"Er, OK," Blue T-shirt said. "Hey, Franco!" he called to the truck driver. "There's some stuff in the back I can't reach. Fetch it out for me, will you?"

"Do you remember anyone coming in yesterday, asking about kittens?" Andi repeated, shifting the box so that she had a better grip as they shuffled back inside the shop.

"We can put it down here," Blue T-shirt said, nodding to a clear space on the floor. "Kittens, you say? Yeah, there was someone who wanted to buy stuff for a new kitten."

Nina staggered into the shop and almost tripped over the doormat, since she was completely unable to see her feet over the stack of pet beds. Andi reached her just in time to stop the beds from toppling on to the floor, and helped her set them down by the till.

"What were they like?" Andi prompted, turning back to Blue T-shirt who was stacking cans of pet food on to a shelf.

"Who?" Blue T-shirt reached into the box for some more cans.

"The people who came into the shop and asked about kittens." Andi shot a frustrated glance at Nina.

Blue T-shirt shrugged. "They came in, they bought blankets and droppers, they left. I didn't get much of a look at them."

"Did you get their names?" Nina asked hopefully.

Blue T-shirt straightened up. "What is this, twenty questions?" he grumbled. "We didn't introduce ourselves. They paid cash and left. Now, can I get back to work?"

Nina was about to ask another question, but Andi laid a hand on her shoulder. This wasn't getting them anywhere. "Well, thanks anyway," she said, struggling to keep the disappointment out of her voice. "Sorry we bothered you."

As they were heading out of the shop, Blue T-shirt called them back. "I don't know if it's helpful," he said, "but they had some kind of accent. You know, like British or something? A bit like yours actually."

Andi whirled round. "British?" she echoed in astonishment. She'd heard a British accent recently, hadn't she? Yes – the Tatfords! Could they have something to do with the kittens' disappearance?

"Let's call Mom and ask her if the Tatfords came into the shop yesterday," Nina said, as they hurried back towards Santa Rosa Crafts.

Andi linked arms with her. "And maybe Tate will have come home by now," she suggested.

But back at the shop, there was still no sign of the old dog. Mr Nelson was calmly arranging a stack of rugs as they came through the door.

"Hi, you two," he said. "What do you think of this display? Too much red? Should I mix it up a little more?"

Andi was puzzled. She knew Mr Nelson loved his dog. So why was he acting as though nothing had happened? He hadn't even asked if they'd seen him.

If Nina was troubled by the way her grandfather was behaving, she gave no sign. "We have a new lead on the kittens, Grandfather!" she said. "Can I call Mom and ask her something?"

"Of course," said Mr Nelson. "Perhaps you could give me a hand arranging the window, Andi."

Andi wanted to ask Mr Nelson how he was feeling about Tate, but she suddenly felt shy and couldn't work out the right way to ask. Instead, she busied herself lifting the rugs and draping them over one another until they made a beautiful fan of colour.

Nina hung up the phone. "The Tatfords did come in!" she said. "Mom says she definitely remembers their British accents. They browsed a while, but the phone rang out back and when Mom returned from answering it, they had gone."

"What time was that?" Andi asked.

"About four o'clock," Nina replied.

Everything was fitting into place! The kittens had still been in the shop at three-thirty – the blonde woman at the Sunny Inn had been positive about the time. But one major thing was worrying Andi. The Tatfords had seemed so nice! Could they really be kitten thieves?

"You can never tell what people are truly like when you only meet them once," Nina said, guessing what Andi was thinking. "Come on, we'd better get over to the campsite. We have to talk to them!"

Andi gasped. "But we can't! The campsite man said they left last night for the Grand Canyon!" She stared at Nina in dismay. "What are we going to do now?"

Chapter Ten

"I seem to have a knack for appearing at the wrong moment." Mr Talbot was standing in the doorway, holding his car keys. "What's wrong? You two look like you've seen a ghost."

"Everything's wrong!" Andi burst out. "We just keep reaching dead ends, Dad. We think we know who took the kittens, but if we're right, they've already left town and taken the kittens with them. The only way we'll find them now is if someone is prepared to drive us all the way to the Grand Canyon. As if *that's* going to happen."

Mr Talbot looked astonished. "You found out who took the kittens?"

"We're as sure as we can be," Andi said. "I mean, we don't have any proof, but we've checked everything else and it just *fits*."

"You can't accuse people without proof," Mr Talbot warned. "Do they have a motive?"

"No," Andi said helplessly. "Unless you count how cute the kittens are. We've been following the trail all day. We checked out a lead that took us to the motel, then the campsite, then to the hardware shop in town, then to the pet shop and now back here. We were *this* close, Dad." She held up her thumb and forefinger close together.

Mr Talbot looked dumbfounded. "You followed that whole chain of clues? And this is where you ended up? It sounds like your theory is worth pursuing, then."

Andi shrugged. "Not if the kittens have gone all the way to the Grand Canyon. They might as well be on the moon for all the chance we've got of finding them now."

Mr Talbot came over and rested his hands on Andi's shoulders. "I'm very proud of you, Andi," he said. "Coming this far has taken a lot of persistence and brainpower. I can't believe you didn't give up." He paused and gave a wry smile. "Well actually, I can. You're as stubborn as your dad when you put your mind to it, aren't you?"

Andi forced a smile. "I suppose I must be." She

turned to Nina. "Sorry it turned out like this. I really thought we'd find them, you know?"

"That's OK," Nina said. "You did your best. I would have given up ages ago."

"Who's giving up?" Mr Talbot demanded. "You need someone to drive you to the Grand Canyon? I'll do it."

Andi stared at him. "But it's three hundred miles away!" she protested. "Haven't you got a meeting this afternoon?"

"I'll call and postpone it," Mr Talbot said, digging in his pocket for his mobile phone.

"You'd do that for me?" Andi said in disbelief. "So I can find some kittens?"

Mr Talbot looked up from keying in the number. "That's what dads are for," he said simply. "Your dedication has really impressed me, Andi. You've shown logic, and common sense, and most of all, persistence. That's worth at least three hundred miles in my book."

A lump swelled in Andi's throat, so big that it threatened to choke her. "Dad—" she began, but Nina interrupted.

"The guy with the ponytail at the campsite reception said the Tatfords were going to take it easy along the way. We might not have to go as far as the

Grand Canyon after all. Right, I'll make sandwiches and fill some water bottles. Oh, and we need a map! We're really going after them? I can't believe it! Mr Talbot, you're the best!"

Andi smiled. *Just what I was going to say*, she thought.

"Are you going to stay overnight somewhere?" Mr Nelson asked, stepping down from the window as Nina dashed back to the kitchen.

Mr Talbot shook his head. "I can only take the rest of today off. Hopefully we'll catch them up if they're in a motor home, but if for any reason we need to drive through to the Grand Canyon itself, we'll just have to get back pretty late."

"In that case, we'd better get moving!" Andi exclaimed, checking her watch. "It's gone eleven already."

"The Tatfords will probably be taking it slow, like Nina said," Mr Nelson said. "You should check all the campsites along the way, in case you end up overtaking them. And there's a new campsite a couple of hours out of town – it won't be on your map because it only opened last month. It's by a waterfall. Make sure you check it out."

Andi nodded and made a note on the back of an old shop receipt.

Nina brought out a rucksack full of food and bottled drinks. She also pulled out the cardboard box and blanket from under the kitchen table, in case they really did find the kittens and needed a safe way to bring them home. Then, after Andi's dad had finished his phone call and they'd said goodbye to Mr Nelson, Nina and Andi followed him out to the Jeep.

"They would have taken this road first, up to Flagstaff." Nina pointed to the map.

"Here we go, then," Mr Talbot declared, and swung out into the road.

Soon the dusty sprawl of Tucson was behind them and the Jeep was powering north along the wide desert road. Mr Talbot put on the radio, but unlike the trip to the Canyon de Chelly, Nina and Andi were too busy planning the route to sing along to the songs.

"It looks as though there are campsites here and here," Andi said, pointing to the symbols on the map.

"We mustn't forget the new place Grandfather mentioned, the one with the waterfall," said Nina. "I hope it's signed off the highway."

Andi stared out of the window. Cacti decorated the landscape, their spiny arms stretched out, just like they did in cowboy films, and she remembered that she still had to buy a cactus for her new room. The time she had spent with her dad painting the furniture felt like a lifetime ago.

"Look, there's a diner coming up!" Nina shaded her eyes against the sun. "Maybe the Tatfords stopped off for something to eat?"

"Good idea, but there are no motor homes in the car lot," said Mr Talbot. "If they stopped here, they're long gone by now."

Sure enough, the car park contained only two or three battered pick-up trucks and another Jeep like Mr Talbot's. They drove straight past, on and on through the desert. They passed a small shop and a petrol pump. Andi didn't see a single person at either place. It was as if they had all been blown away by the wind.

They ate their sandwiches on the move, and crunched through some juicy green apples. At last, they saw a new-looking sign to a campsite.

"This must be the one with the waterfall," Nina said, studying the map as Mr Talbot turned off the main road and they bumped along down a pitted concrete road. "The river's marked here, see? If the Tatfords stayed anywhere last night, this will be it."

After jolting along the road for a couple of miles, they found themselves on a grassy river bank. There were a few trees by the water's edge, and shade was provided by a craggy cliff. A spectacular waterfall cascaded down the cliff face into a dark-blue pool. Several camper vans and tents were grouped around the pool, and one or two people were swimming.

"It's beautiful!" Andi exclaimed. She thought longingly about diving in as they climbed out of the Jeep.

"I'm afraid we can't stop for long," Mr Talbot warned. "Twenty minutes maximum."

Andi forced her mind back to the missing kittens. She and Nina ran into the campsite. At first glance, the campers all looked the same. Were they going to have to knock on every single door? If the Tatfords weren't here, they didn't have a moment to waste. They needed some kind of clue – anything . . .

"Andi!" Nina squeaked, pointing. "Look at that flag!"

The distinctive red, white and blue design of the Union Jack flag hung in the window of a large camper parked in the shade of the cliff. Andi and Nina raced towards it – and stopped dead when they saw a little girl, aged about five, sitting on the steps.

"Er, hello," Andi said uncertainly. "Is your name Tatford?"

The little girl stared at them. "Mummy!" she called. "Someone's here to talk to you!"

Mummy? Andi frowned. Jane Tatford had looked too old to have a daughter this young.

"What's the matter, darling?" A dark-haired woman in a rainbow-coloured blouse put her head out of the camper van. She had an English accent. "Oh, hello. Can I help?"

It wasn't Jane Tatford. Although Andi wasn't really surprised, she couldn't stop her heart plummeting into her trainers.

"I'm sorry to disturb you," she said. "We're looking for an English couple called Tatford. Do you know if there are any other English people on this campsite?"

The woman shook her head. "We've only just arrived," she said. "I'm pretty sure we're the only English people here. Sorry."

Just in case she was wrong, Andi and Nina searched the rest of the campsite for a camper van with some kind of British clue in its window – or three adorable kittens. But it was clear that the Tatfords weren't there.

"That's too bad," Mr Talbot said as Andi and Nina climbed back into the Jeep. "Hang in there, guys. Maybe we'll have better luck at the next site."

Andi reached over and squeezed his shoulder. Even though she was desperately worried about the kittens, it felt great to be pet-finding with her dad!

They drove out of the campsite and back on to the road, which shimmered in the afternoon heat. They travelled in silence through the rock-strewn landscape. There wasn't another car in sight. The scenery was dramatic and desolate now, with craggy mountains rising on either side.

Up ahead, Andi caught the flash of a reflector band. Three workmen in hard hats were sitting in the back of their lorry, which was parked at an angle across the road.

Mr Talbot slowed the Jeep as one of the men hopped off the back of the lorry and waved.

"Sorry," the workman said. "You can't get through this way."

"What do you mean, we can't get through?" Andi gasped. "We've got to get to the Grand Canyon!"

The workman tipped back his hat. "Maybe you do, but you'll have to go the long way round," he said. "There's been a rock fall. We're working on it, but this section of the highway is closed until tomorrow morning. You'll have to take this road instead, and rejoin the highway further up." He pointed to a small road leading off to the left.

"But this goes up into the mountains," Nina said, dismayed. "It could take hours to get back to the highway and the Tatfords could be way ahead of us by then."

"It looks like we don't have a choice," Mr Talbot pointed out. "Let's hope that the Tatfords had to come this way too."

They followed the new road as it twisted up through crags and bluffs, the Jeep's engine grinding in a low gear for much of the way. When they reached the top of the incline, the view across the desert made them all gasp. Andi stared at the road snaking on the far side of the rock fall like a thin grey thread, but she couldn't see anything that looked like a camper van. Perhaps the campsite manager had been wrong. Perhaps the Tatfords were in a hurry to get to the Grand Canyon after all.

The road grew increasingly narrow and rocky, and soon they found themselves driving so close to the edge of a cliff that Andi had to close her eyes.

"This can't be right," Mr Talbot muttered, bringing the Jeep to a halt and reaching for the map. "We seem to be heading further and further from the highway. We should have seen another sign by now."

"It's four o'clock already," Nina said desperately. "At this rate we'll have to turn round and go back to

Tucson before we reach the Canyon. What are we going to do?"

Straight ahead of them, the road forked in two. There was a sign on the right-hand fork.

SCULPTURE GALLERY
NATIVE CRAFTS
Hand-thrown salt glaze pots for sale

Andi stared at the sign for a few moments. There was something about the words that made her fingers tingle. Was it the line about sculpture, or salt glaze pots?

Yes, that was it!

"Dad, we've got to take the right-hand fork," she said. "Mr Tatford was really interested in the pottery at Santa Rosa Crafts, remember?"

"Yes! He talked about a salt glaze," Nina recalled, looking at Andi with a flash of hope in her eyes.

Mr Talbot checked his watch. "We've already lost an hour on this diversion," he warned. "It doesn't say how far this gallery is. Are you sure you want to check it out?"

"It's just a hunch," Andi admitted, "but we've come this far. I say we risk it."

Mr Talbot nodded. "Whatever you say, boss," he

murmured, and turned the Jeep to follow the sign for the gallery.

They bumped down the rutted road. After ten minutes, Andi spotted a square wooden building nestled into the mountainside, surrounded by forests. Large sculptures in rock and bronze and strange, twisted pieces of wood stood beneath the trees.

Mr Talbot slowed the Jeep and turned a corner into a small car park. A sparkling white camper van was tucked up against the gallery building, and fluttering on a clothes line beside it were two Disney World T-shirts and three pairs of white socks.

"Man, tacky T-shirts," Nina murmured, shading her eyes. "Those have to belong to tourists."

"That camper's got a Miami number plate!" Andi said, recognizing the Florida colours. A rush of hope flooded through her. "The Tatfords said they started their holiday in Miami!"

The camper's rear window was just above the number plate. Three tiny fluffy shapes bundled against the glass, their little pink mouths opening and closing in silent meows.

"It's them!" Andi yelled, scrambling out of the Jeep.

"I can see Nascha!" Nina said, racing after Andi

towards the camper. "Look, in the window! And there's Dezba – and Yas too. Andi, we've found them!"

Chapter Eleven

The kittens stood up curiously with their paws against the glass and stared at them.

"It's really them!" Nina said, half crying and half laughing. "I can't believe we found them!"

Andi felt slightly dazed as she peered into the dim interior of the Tatfords' camper. A few minutes ago, they'd been lost in the mountains with no sign of the Tatfords or the missing kittens anywhere. Then she'd followed a hunch about Mr Tatford's love of pottery, and now they were standing in a hidden mountain valley, hundreds of miles from Tucson, staring at precisely what they'd come to find.

"How are we going to get them out of there?" she asked.

Nina tried the door of the camper van. It was unlocked. "Simple," she declared. "The Tatfords stole them from us, so we're going to go in there and steal them back!"

"You can't!" Andi warned, putting a hand on Nina's shoulder as she began to climb up the steps. "You're not thinking straight, Nina. You can't just walk into someone's camper as if you own it! We'd better wait for the Tatfords to come back, and then we can ask them what they're doing with the kittens."

"You're absolutely right, Andi," Mr Talbot said, walking over to join them. "There's probably a perfectly rational explanation, and we owe it to the Tatfords to hear them out."

Reluctantly, Nina let go of the door handle. They all looked at the kittens in the window again. Nascha was still leaning up against the glass, her mouth open in a plaintive mew. Dezba and Yas had gone to sleep, curled up together in a tangle of tabby-and-white fur.

"Jim, look who it is!" a voice exclaimed behind her. "It's the girls from that lovely craft shop!"

Andi spun round. Jim and Jane Tatford were walking across the grass towards them. Andi searched their faces for signs of guilt or embarrassment, but they just looked surprised.

"This is a most extraordinary coincidence,"

Jim Tatford declared. "Have you come to look at the pots?"

Andi was floored. They were supposed to look guilty, not happy to see them! "Er, we came to get the kittens back," she said awkwardly.

Jane Tatford looked confused. "You want them *back*?" she said. "But I thought you wanted to get rid of them."

It was Nina's turn to look surprised. "We never said that," she protested.

Everyone started talking at once. Mr Tatford waved his arms for silence. "I think you'd better come inside for a cup of tea," he said. "It looks as though we've all got our wires crossed."

Inside, the camper was cosy and comfortable, with plush carpeting and soft tartan seats. Dezba and Nascha immediately jumped down from the window and padded over to say hello, while Yas stayed snoozing on the sill. Nina and Andi knelt on the seat to play with them, laughing as Dezba pounced on their fingers. Mrs Tatford switched on the kettle and Mr Tatford found some biscuits in one of the tiny cupboards.

"I don't know what to say." Mr Tatford looked rather flustered as he passed round a plate of biscuits. "We thought we'd be doing you a favour by taking the kittens off your hands. Your grandfather talked about getting rid of them!"

"He only meant we should take them out of the shop to the living room at the back," Andi explained.

"We understood that with the mother cat out of the picture, it was only a matter of time before the kittens were in danger from snakes and coyotes," Mrs Tatford put in anxiously. "When we went back to the shop, the lady in there was so rushed off her feet that we felt we had to do something to help. So we took the kittens. Didn't you see our note?"

"You left a note?" Nina asked in surprise.

"Yes, on a stack of rugs by the door." Mrs Tatford frowned. "Gosh, how dreadful for you if you never got it."

"It must have blown out of the door!" Andi guessed. "Your mum said it was a windy day, Nina."

"Oh, I'm so sorry." Mrs Tatford looked appalled. "What must you have thought of us?"

"We didn't know what to think," Andi said, deciding it would be tactful not to admit the conclusion they'd jumped to.

Mr Tatford was still looking confused. "But, Nina,

you said something about not being able to keep them for ever, didn't you? So what's going to happen to them?"

"I love them dearly, but it's not up to me if they stay at the shop," Nina said. "I have to respect their wild nature. Their mother will come back one day, and then the kittens will decide if they want to follow her back to the desert. It's their choice, however much I want them to stay with me for ever. But I would never leave them in danger! I'm going to keep them inside until they are older, and then I'll let them run in the yard at night, just so they get used to the idea." She swallowed. "I have to give them the chance to leave, even though it breaks my heart."

Mrs Tatford reached over and patted her hand. "I'm really sorry for making you unhappy. I never dreamt that the kittens meant this much to you!"

"What were you going to do with them at the end of your holiday?" Andi asked the Tatfords.

"Take them home with us, hopefully," Mr Tatford said. "We've got friends who brought a cat over from America, and she dealt with the quarantine regulations very well. We thought we could do the same with these three."

There were certainly plenty of signs that the

Tatfords knew how to take care of cats. Andi spotted a clean litter tray in one corner and there was a comfortable fleece-lined basket under the table.

"We're big supporters of global animal charities," Mrs Tatford went on, picking up Yas and stroking his golden tummy. "Giving these kittens a home seemed like the right thing to do at the time."

"I'm so sorry about the misunderstanding," Nina apologized, "but we'd really like to take them home. The kittens are wanted, I promise. I'm so sorry I didn't make that clear."

Mrs Tatford blinked, as if she was trying not to cry. "Of course you must take them," she said. "I can see now that we completely misread the situation. We'll miss them terribly, but I know you've got their best interests at heart." She pulled a tissue from her sleeve and blew her nose.

"And they have been quite restless cooped up in here," Mr Tatford confessed, scooping Nascha up off the floor and handing her to Andi. "They'll be happier back in the shop, with room to play."

"However did you find us?" Mrs Tatford asked. "We camped in the desert last night, and you can't see this gallery from that little mountain road. I still can't believe you're here!"

"Andi's great at following clues," Nina told her. "We tracked down the pet shop where you bought supplies for the kittens, then followed you on the road to the Grand Canyon because we knew that was where you were going next. When we got diverted off the main road, we saw that sign and remembered Mr Tatford talking about a salt glaze on one of our pots."

"Goodness!" Mr Tatford looked astounded. "Fancy remembering something like that! You two should be private detectives."

Andi smiled. "Well, I belong to the Pet Finders Club in Lancaster," she said. "We do this kind of thing all the time – finding pets, I mean. Not following people across the desert!"

Mr Talbot grinned at her. "Just as well. I can't see your mum would be too happy if you made this a regular feature!" He glanced at his watch. "We need to get going. Do you think these little ones are ready to leave?" He nodded towards the kittens.

"I guess so!" said Nina, cuddling Nascha close to her chin.

Mr Talbot went to fetch the cardboard box from the Jeep. The Tatfords helped to settle the kittens on the blanket inside before Andi carefully carried the box out of the camper van.

"You must take this," said Mrs Tatford, handing Nina the fleece-lined pet bed and a shopping bag containing a packet of kitten food and two empty bowls. "It'll only take up room in the van."

"Oh thank you!" Nina said. "They'll love this bed. We're really, really sorry about the mix-up. You've been so understanding, and I can see that the kittens mean a lot to you."

"Such is life," Mr Tatford said bravely. "We shouldn't have taken them. I'm so sorry you didn't see the note, and I'm sorry you had to come all this way to retrieve them. Perhaps we could stay in touch by email? We'd love to hear how the kittens are getting on."

"I'll send you photos," Nina promised, writing down the Tatfords' email address on an old envelope.

"You will take care of them, won't you?" Mrs Talbot said, with a catch in her voice as Andi loaded the box of kittens into the Jeep.

"Don't worry," Andi said with a smile, climbing in beside the kittens and leaning out of the window to say goodbye. Next to her, Dezba butted the flaps on the box with her head, looking for a way out. "If Dezba ever meets a coyote, I think it's the coyote who'll be in trouble!"

* * *

The journey back to Tucson seemed to be much shorter than the outward trip, but it was still almost sunset by the time they reached Santa Rosa Crafts. Mr Talbot parked the Jeep outside and helped Andi and Nina to carry the box of wriggling kittens into the shop. Nina undid the flaps and the kittens tumbled out one after the other, sniffing excitedly at all the familiar smells.

"I can't believe you found them!" Angie exclaimed, hugging Nina and Andi both at the same time. "We'd never have got them back if it hadn't been for you, Andi. We can't thank you enough."

Mr Talbot put his arm round Andi and pulled her close. "I'm really proud of you," he said softly. "The way you kept looking for the kittens, even though you must have felt like giving up a lot of the time – that's really something, Andi. Everyone is lucky you've started your Pet Finders Club."

Andi hugged him back. "It was a pretty wild desert dash," she joked. "And I think you must be an official Pet Finder now, Dad. Welcome to the club."

Mr Nelson walked down the shop towards them. Nina flew into his arms and he kissed her on the top of her head. "I see that you found those rascals," he commented. "They look bigger, and

I'm sure they will be twice as much trouble."

"You don't fool me, Grandfather," Nina scolded. "You're as happy to see them as I am. And they'll quiet down as they get older, I promise."

"Is there any news of Tate?" Andi asked hopefully. "Now we've found the kittens, we can really concentrate on looking for him," she added. "We'll do some more posters. And door-to-door questioning! Everyone knows him round here. There are bound to be some really great leads."

Mr Nelson rested his dark eyes on her. "Come with me, both of you," he said, holding out his hands. "I have something to show you both."

Nina gazed at her grandfather. "You have bad news, don't you?" she said in a trembling voice. "I can tell from your face."

Dakota led Andi and Nina into the back garden behind the shop. The crimson sun was hanging low in the sky, spreading warm coppery light through the clouds. "You need no gold when you have the sunset. It is riches in itself. I am happy to know that the sky is full of my ancestors. And I am happy that Tate is with them now.'

Andi felt her heart miss a beat.

"Mr Hobson called me," Mr Nelson went on. "He

found Tate's body underneath a bush in his yard."

"Dead?" Nina whispered.

Dakota nodded. "He was an old dog, Nina. He'd had a good long life and he didn't suffer any pain."

"But he died on his own!" Nina protested, tears welling in her eyes. "That wouldn't have happened if we'd found him in time. No one should die alone."

'Dogs share many things with their ancestors, the wolves," Mr Nelson said. "Wolves choose to leave the pack when it is their time to die. It is nature's way."

Andi's heart felt like it was breaking. She didn't trust herself to speak, so she just reached out and held Nina's hand.

"Tate knew that his life was at its end," Mr Nelson said gently. "Think how he has been slowing down recently. I could see in his eyes that he was ready to leave us, and I was just waiting for him to go for a walk one day and not come back. There was nothing I could have done to stop him – and it would not have been fair to try. He wanted to die outside, in the world that he loved so much."

Tears rushed into Andi's eyes, blurring her vision. "I'm sorry, Mr Nelson," she choked out. "So sorry."

"It is the natural way of things," Mr Nelson said. He pointed at the flaming sun. "Tate's spirit is in the sky now, hunting cloud rabbits and running with the wind. There is a Navajo song that explains it better than I can. I will translate it for you." And he began to sing:

When it comes your time to die,
Be not like those whose hearts
Are filled with fear of death,
So that when their time comes
They weep and pray for a little more time
To live their lives over again
In a different way.
Sing your death song and
Die like a hero going home.

Mr Nelson let the last note hang in the air. As if the sun had heard his song, it disappeared abruptly behind the mountains and darkness swept over the desert like a raven's wing.

Andi's eyes swam with tears. Tate was the first pet she hadn't found. Everything Mr Nelson had said, everything in the beautiful song, rang true, but it was a bitter truth all the same.

Andi spent the last day of her holiday with her dad, putting the finishing touches to her room. She had found the perfect cactus at the local garden centre, and it looked great in the corner of her room. Then she and her dad had gone shopping for New Year's presents for Andi's mum and friends back in Aldcliffe. Andi had found two fantastic masks – a rattlesnake and a fairy – that she planned to give to Tristan and Natalie to wear at Tristan's New Year's Eve party. She'd found one for herself too – a tabby cat mask, to remind her of Mosi's kittens. She got a scented candle for her mum and bought her dad a set of paints. "So you can take those art lessons you mentioned," she explained as she gave them to him.

Mr Talbot was delighted. "No more excuses!" he agreed, examining the rows of coloured squares in the tin. Andi could see that he was already planning a painting in his mind. She hoped it wasn't going to be entirely blue.

Now, at last, it was time to head for the airport. Andi stared round the little room, trying to imprint the colourful blankets, the yellow cushions and the blue furniture, the green baskets and the incense burner on the windowsill on to her mind. She'd never found a rug – perhaps because in her heart, she knew the tree-of-life rug would have been perfect.

"You must remember to water the cactus," she told her dad, shouldering her bag.

"Cacti don't need water," her dad pointed out with a grin. "That's why they live in deserts, remember?"

"OK, but you have to dust its leaves. Promise?" Andi begged. She hugged her dad tightly. "I've had such a good time," she said, resting her head on his shoulder. "Thanks for everything, Dad. You're the best." She really meant it. She couldn't wait to see her mum and Buddy again, but it was sad having to leave her dad and this magical place behind.

Her dad hugged her back. "Come and see me again soon," he said. "Maybe next time we'll get to the Grand Canyon, hey? Without having to chase any missing kittens on the way." His eyes were twinkling, but Andi didn't mind him teasing her any more. He understood what pet-finding meant to her now.

They passed Santa Rosa Crafts on the way to the airport, and Andi asked her dad to let her call in and say goodbye to the Nelsons. The kittens raced up to the door and tumbled around her feet, watched indulgently by Dakota who was standing by the till.

"Careful, little one!" Andi laughed at Dezba, who was trying to nip her ankles. "Are you a cat or a tiger cub?" She stroked Nascha's pale, pretty head and tickled Yas on his golden tummy for the last time. This had been one of the most amazing pet hunts

ever. Andi cast her mind over the long, twisting trail of clues, misunderstandings and mountain roads that had finally led them to the kittens over two hundred miles from where they started. It was incredible that they'd found them at all!

And Tate – Andi swallowed as she thought of the gentle old hunting dog. As Mr Nelson said, it had been his time to die, like a hero going home. It was important to remember Tate's long happy life, not his death.

"I have a gift for you," Nina said shyly, coming through the beaded curtain with something held behind her back. "To say thank you for everything and so you don't forget about us."

To Andi's delight, Nina was holding a silver squash blossom necklace. The Navajo girl reached out and put it round Andi's neck, where it felt warm and heavy.

"Thank you!" Andi exclaimed. "It's beautiful. But really, you don't need to thank me. And there's no way I'll ever forget you!"

"And I have something to give you, too," said Mr Nelson. "You loved this and so now it is yours."

Andi stared in astonishment as Nina's grandfather reached behind the counter and handed her the beautiful tree-of-life rug. "I don't know what to say," she stammered. "Thank you doesn't seem enough."

Mr Nelson smiled. "It is plenty," he said. "Go safely, and visit us again soon."

"I will," Andi promised.

There was a hoarse, unkitten-like meow at the back of the shop. They all turned. Andi saw a thin sand-coloured cat standing warily in the kitchen, looking through the beaded curtain at them. It was the cat she'd seen on her very first evening in Tucson.

"Mosi!" Nina gasped. "Boy, are we glad to see you! Your kittens have been such troublemakers . . ."

book 8:

THE PET FINDERS CLUB

Dachshund in Danger

Do you love animals?
Has your pet ever gone missing?

Well meet Andi, Tristan and Natalie – The Pet Finders Club. Animals don't stay lost for long with them hot on the trail!

The Pet Finders have fallen in love with some newborn miniature dachshunds. Especially one called Koko. But the next time they visit he's acting like a completely different dog...
It's a real puzzle and the Pet Finders can only think of one answer:

Koko's been switched!